With shaking hands, she unzipped her bag and reached inside for Cole's wallet.

Cole stared back at her from a California driver's license. He hadn't lied about being a California boy. Ignoring the cash in the billfold, she jammed her fingers into the slot behind his license and pulled out a stack of cards.

The gold-embossed letters on the top card blurred before her eyes and she slid down the length of the door until she was crouching against it.

Cole Pierson was a DEA agent, and he must be looking for the woman he believed murdered Johnny Diamond and stole his drug money.

He was looking for her.

IN THE ARMS OF THE ENEMY

CAROL ERICSON

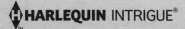

For all my SHS friends

Recycling programs
for this product may
not exist in your area.

ISBN-13: 978-0-373-69941-4

In the Arms of the Enemy

Copyright © 2016 by Carol Ericson

Printed in U.S.A.

Carol Ericson is a bestselling, award-winning author of more than forty books. She has an eerie fascination for true-crime stories, a love of film noir and a weakness for reality TV, all of which fuel her imagination to create her own tales of murder, mayhem and mystery. To find out more about Carol and her current projects, please visit her website at www.carolericson.com, "where romance flirts with danger."

Books by Carol Ericson

Harlequin Intrigue

Target: Timberline

Single Father Sheriff
Sudden Second Chance
Army Ranger Redemption
In the Arms of the Enemy

Brothers in Arms: Retribution

Under Fire
The Pregnancy Plot
Navy SEAL Spy
Secret Agent Santa

Brody Law

The Bridge
The District
The Wharf
The Hill

Harlequin Intrigue Noir

Toxic

Visit the Author Profile page at Harlequin.com for more titles.

CAST OF CHARACTERS

Caroline Johnson—A woman with no memory, no ID and a dead body in her motel room, "Caroline" finds herself at the center of drug trafficking and a twenty-five-year-old kidnapping.

Cole Pierson—A DEA agent whose longtime quarry winds up dead at the hands of a mysterious female. His quest for the suspect leads him to Caroline, but he can't determine if she's a killer or an innocent woman caught up in events beyond her control.

Johnny Diamond—This drug dealer's death by poisoning sets off a chain of events that will result in the culmination of an explosive case of kidnapping and drug trafficking.

Linda Gunderson—Her loyalty to Caroline is based on a lie, but she stands beside her new friend in the face of increasing danger.

Dr. Jules Shipman—This therapist wants to help her new patient, Caroline, regain her memories, but someone doesn't want Dr. Shipman to do her job.

Rocky Whitecotton—A member of the Quileute tribe, this rebel bucked the traditions of his people twenty-five years ago when he turned to drug dealing for a nefarious purpose and now he needs Caroline to keep her mouth shut—or he'll shut it for her.

Jason Foster—A Quileute whose uncle ran with Rocky in the old days, he's going to have to decide where his loyalties lie or pay the price.

James Brice—The brother of Heather Brice, one of the Timberline Trio, returns to Timberline to settle some family business.

The Timberline Trio—Kayla Rush, Stevie Carson and Heather Brice were snatched from Timberline twenty-five years ago. The truth of their disappearance will rock Timberline.

Chapter One

Her head throbbed as she stared at the dead guy. He had to be dead. She zeroed in on his chest, watching for the rise and fall of his breathing. Nothing.

Dried foam clung to his parted lips and chin in silvery trails, clinging to his beard like gossamer spiderwebs. His open, bloodshot eyes bugged out from their sockets like those of a surprised cartoon character.

She checked the carpet around his body—no blood, no weapon, just a plastic water bottle on its side with a quarter of its contents still inside.

She sat back on her heels and massaged her temples, which now throbbed as much as the back of her head. What had happened in this cheap motel room? Who was he?

Who was she?

A sob bubbled in her throat. That terror had slammed into her head-on before she even saw the body on the floor, when she'd come to, lying diagonally across the bed, fully clothed. She'd put that problem on the back burner when she noticed the dead guy, but a complete memory loss couldn't be ignored forever.

There had to be a clue to her identity somewhere. She rose to her feet, her gaze sweeping the room, with its upended lamp, disheveled double bed and cracked picture frame above that bed.

The dead man hadn't gone down without a fight. With her? Had she killed this man in a fight?

She took in his large frame sprawled on the threadbare carpet and shook her head. Hard to believe. But then maybe—she glanced at her toes, painted with pale pink polish—she was some ninja amazon woman.

A hysterical laugh crackled through the room and she clapped a hand over her mouth. She didn't like the sound of that laugh. Wrapping her arms around her midsection, she tiptoed toward the open door of the bathroom. She held her breath and flicked the light switch with her knuckle.

At least no more dead bodies greeted her. She shuffled toward the chipped vanity and slowly raised her head to face the mirror.

She gasped. Leaning forward, she traced the outline of a red spot forming high on her cheekbone, beneath her right eye. Then she rubbed the painful area on the back of her head, her fingers circling a huge lump. Had she and the man gotten into a brawl?

She stepped back, studying the fine-boned face in the mirror, a slim column of a neck and a pair of narrow shoulders encased in a flimsy T-shirt. That slip of a thing that stared back at her with wide eyes couldn't have taken down a kitten, never mind a full-grown man.

She bit her bottom lip and winced. She hunched forward and dabbed at the lip she now saw was swol-

len. The dead guy had done a number on her before…
succumbing. But what had he succumbed from?

Maybe someone had attacked them both and left
her for dead. Maybe that someone would return. She
backed away from the mirror and stumbled out of the
small bathroom.

The walls of the dumpy motel room closed in on her
all at once and she listed to the side like a drunken sailor
on the deck of a ship. Reaching out a hand to clutch the
faded bedspread, she sank to the edge of the bed. She
should call the police, 911.

Her gaze traveled to the inert form on the floor and
she shivered. Unless she'd killed him.

She crept to the window, where she hooked a finger
between two slats of the blinds and peeked outside. She
squinted into the gray light. The green numbers on the
digital clock by the bed had already told her it was just
after six thirty in the morning.

A small, dark car huddled in a parking space in front
of the room. Could it be theirs? His? Hers?

She patted the pockets of her jeans—no keys, no ID,
no money. She gulped back her rising panic and lunged
for the closet. She swung open the door and jumped
back as a small wheeled suitcase fell over on its side,
just missing her bare toes.

Dropping to her knees, she scrabbled for the zipper
with trembling hands. When she flipped open the suitcase, she plunged her hands into a pile of clothes—her
clothes. She'd packed in a hurry.

She pushed the bag away from her and crawled on
her hands and knees to peer under the bed. Nothing

but dust occupied the space and she sneezed as it tickled her nose.

What woman didn't carry a purse with her?

She searched the rest of the room, giving the body on the floor a wide berth. She ended in the middle of the room, hands on her hips.

One place left she hadn't searched. She slid a sideways glance at the dead man, and then pivoted toward the bathroom. She yanked a hand towel from the rack. She returned to the man and crouched beside him. With the towel covering her hand, she tugged at his jacket, which fell open, exposing his neck and an intricate tattoo curling around it and down his chest. Vines, barbwire, a skull and the letters *L* and *C* intertwined. LC. Larry?

She rifled Larry's front pockets and heard the jingle of the keys before she saw them. She closed her fingers, still wrapped in the towel, around a key chain and pulled it free of Larry's pocket. She cupped the keys in her palm, frowning at the yellow daisy key chain— didn't seem like Larry's style at all. Maybe the car belonged to her.

A pair of boots, socks stuffed inside, was lined up near the door of the motel room, and she put them on—a perfect fit, kind of like Cinderella in an alternate universe. She eased open the door and pressed her eye to the crack.

Luckily for her, the motel didn't seem to be a hotspot of tourist activity or any other kind of activity—except for in this room. She swung the door wide and stepped into a cool, damp blast of air. Tucking her chin to her chest, she scurried to the compact car and jabbed at the key fob hooked to the key chain.

The lights of the little car flashed once in greeting, and she blew out a breath. She dropped onto the front seat and slid down. Then she pulled open the glove compartment, and a stack of napkins tumbled out.

Leaving them where they fell, she plunged her hand into the glove box and started pulling papers out, glancing at each one before tossing it to the floor.

When she found the car's registration, she ran a finger across the printed words and read aloud, her voice filling the car, startling her. "Hazel McTavish."

The dead man in the hotel room didn't look like a Hazel. Could she be Hazel? Hazel lived in Seattle, Washington. Was that where she was now? No bells of recognition rang in her head. Seattle meant about as much to her at this point as Timbuktu.

Peering into the back of the car, she scanned the seat and floor. She plucked a black leather jacket from the floor and shook it out. It had to be hers.

With her blood racing, she jammed her hands in the pockets. Her trembling fingers curled around a slip of paper, which she pulled free.

Timberline, WA.

At least there was a common denominator here— Washington. Could she be in Timberline now?

She scooted from the car and locked it with the key fob. She reached into the motel room and yanked the Do Not Disturb sign from the inside door handle, hooking it on the outside before slipping back into the room.

Larry hadn't moved.

Tapping her toe, she assessed the big man on the floor. Did he have a wallet? A phone? He'd landed on his back, and if he kept his wallet in his back pocket, she doubted she could turn him over to do a search.

Her stomach churned. She didn't want to try. Didn't want to touch him.

She had to make some kind of move. She couldn't hang out here until someone came looking for Larry—or her. And where was *here*?

She scurried to the other side of the bed and the telephone on the nightstand. She grabbed a cheap notepad printed with the words *Stardust Motel, Seattle, Washington*, and dropped it.

She returned to the closet and pulled out the suitcase. The clothes in there obviously belonged to her. She wasn't stealing. Her gaze shifted to the dead guy. Theft was the least of her moral concerns right now.

As she slid the door closed, she noticed two bags stacked on the far side of the closet. She parked the suitcase by the front door and dragged open the other closet door.

She unzipped the first duffel bag and peeled back the top, releasing a stream of air between her teeth. Stacks of bills were nestled neatly in the bag, and she clawed through them all the way to the bottom.

Hugging a few thousand dollars to her chest, she stumbled backward until the back of her legs hit the bed. She sat.

What did it all mean? Were she and Larry bank robbers who'd had a disagreement? Lottery winners who couldn't decide how to split their windfall?

She dropped the cash on the floor and returned to the closet. With both hands, she pulled the money duffel off the other one and unzipped the bag on the bottom. This time she swayed and grabbed the closet door to steady herself.

She ran her fingertips along the plastic baggies in the duffel, which looked like they were stuffed with ice chips—but this ice didn't melt. She snatched her hand back from the drugs packaged neatly in the bags.

With her heart hammering in her chest, she swept up the hand towel she'd dropped next to Larry's body and darted around the room, wiping down surfaces from the bathroom to the TV remote to the duffel bags and all the doorknobs and handles in between.

Maybe the dead man had keeled over from a heart attack or a stroke or an aneurysm, but she had no intention of being here when the cops showed up.

She zipped up the drug bag and hoisted the money bag back on top. She gathered the stacks of bills from the floor where she'd dropped them and froze.

She had no purse, no ID, no memory. How could she make her getaway, find herself with no money?

The cash in her hands felt solid, sort of like a crutch, something to hold on to. She needed this money now. If it turned out she was a drug dealer, she'd return it to…someone. She'd pay it back once she discovered her identity.

She stuffed the money into the suitcase by the door and added a few more stacks for good measure. She'd count it later. She'd use just what she needed to get by.

All the excuses she reeled out for herself couldn't

quell the sick feeling in her stomach. She'd make this right, but she couldn't leave her fate to strangers when she didn't even know her own story.

Larry's body emitted a tinny classical tune, and she dropped the money on the floor. She tiptoed toward him and crouched down, clutching the towel in her hand.

A light glowed from the front pocket of his shirt, and she plucked the phone out, using the hand towel. The cell slid off of his body and landed beside his arm.

Squinting, she leaned forward. The display flashed a call from an unknown number, and then went dark. Drug dealers and bank robbers probably didn't store contact names and numbers of their associates in their phones.

Since she was hovering over the body anyway, she swiped at the man's pockets where she'd touched him. She would wipe down the car, take her suitcase and hit the road—first stop Timberline, the name of the town on the slip of paper in her pocket. She was about to rise when a dinging sound stopped her.

The phone lit up again, but this time a text message flashed on the display.

She hunched forward and read the text aloud to the dead man. "'Did you get the girl? Rocky's…'"

In place of an adjective for Rocky's emotion, the texter had inserted a little devil face with smoke coming out his ears. Rocky must be very, very angry.

Was she the girl who had to be gotten? Would've been nice if the texter had used her name to give her a head start on reclaiming her identity.

Cell phones could be tracked. She pushed to her feet

and finished wiping down every possible surface in the room. When she was done, she tucked a corner of the towel in the waistband of her jeans and peeked out the door.

She'd leave the car here—those could be traced, too. She might be Hazel McTavish from Seattle, but she needed to do a little research before stepping into Hazel's life.

But before she left without the car, she wanted to check the trunk first. She'd found a bag of money, a bag of drugs, what next? A bag of weapons?

Poking her head out the door, she cranked it from side to side. The people at this motel didn't seem to be early risers—probably because they were sleeping off the night's activities or had used the room for just a few hours.

She kept her head down and scurried to the compact, unlocking the trunk with the key fob. It sprang open and she used the towel to ease it up.

Chills raced up her spine and her mouth dropped open in a silent scream as her eyes locked on to the vacant stare of her second dead body this morning.

Chapter Two

DEA Agent Cole Pierson turned away from the dead woman's stare. Money, drugs, dead bodies—and he hadn't even officially clocked in yet.

He returned to the motel room, where the odor of decomposing flesh had started to drift through the air. He swiped the back of his hand across his nose. Someone had left the heat blasting in here, which had accelerated the process of the body's breakdown.

Cole still had no problem identifying the deceased—Johnny Diamond. Whatever had happened in this seedy motel room, it couldn't have happened to a more deserving dirtbag.

The King's County Sheriff's Department had descended on the room like a pack of ants at a picnic. One of those ants, Deputy Brookhurst, approached him with a wide grin.

"Quite a haul for you DEA boys, huh? Crank, cash and Johnny Diamond."

"Now we just have to piece together the rest of the puzzle. Where'd he get it, where was he going with it and who were his contacts? Oh yeah, and who offed him?"

With the toe of his boot, Cole prodded the black duffel bag on the floor, containing hundreds of thousands of dollars of methamphetamine, bagged and ready for the street. Then he wedged his hands on his hips and surveyed the room. What had Diamond been doing in this flea trap?

Why risk stealing a car, murdering the owner and stuffing her body in the trunk with this much cash and product on hand? Diamond had been a slick adversary from the day he'd burst onto the drug scene four years ago. He'd managed to keep out of their clutches precisely because he'd avoided missteps like this.

Maybe Diamond had been planning to cash out and head for a tropical island somewhere. Cole smoothed his gloved hands over the pile of money stashed in the other duffel bag and frowned.

"Brookhurst, are you sure your guys didn't touch the cash?"

"Hold on." Brookhurst widened his stance and hooked his thumbs in his pockets like some movie star cowboy. "Are you accusing my boys of something?"

"Stealing? No. Did they move it around? Reposition it? Run their hands through it?" Cole held up his own hands. "Hey, I wouldn't blame 'em."

Brookhurst's puffed-up chest deflated. "I don't think so. Why do you ask?"

Cole traced the uneven grid of the money stacks with his fingertip. "The bills are stuffed into the bag in tight rows, but those rows are messed up at the top—as if someone thumbed through the money. You checked Diamond's pockets?"

"I told you—a set of keys with a flower key chain in the front pocket, wallet in the back pocket. Had maybe a hundred bucks in his wallet."

The county coroners parked a gurney next to Diamond's body. "We're ready to take him if you're done with him."

"Copy us on the autopsy and toxicology reports. You still think it looks like poison?"

One of the coroners held up a plastic bag containing the bottle of water that had been on the floor, and shook it. "Smells like bitter almonds."

Cole whistled. "Cyanide."

"Along with the foaming at the mouth and his reddish skin color, that's my guess. But it's just a guess and we have a lot of tests to run."

"Poison." Cole drummed his fingers against his chin. "The murder weapon of choice for women, but the motel clerk said Diamond checked in as a single."

Brookhurst nudged him and chuckled. "Maybe his old lady mixed up a little something special for him when she caught him cheating, or maybe she was cheating and wanted to bypass the divorce. I should start sniffing the drinks my wife mixes for me."

Cole's jaw tightened and he nodded once. Cheating-spouse jokes didn't hold much humor for him anymore.

Hearing a commotion outside, Cole strode to the door of the motel room. A deputy had stopped two women outside the yellow tape. One of them, speaking

Spanish, kept pointing at the car with the dead body in the trunk.

Cole joined the knot of people. "What's going on, Deputy?"

The officer jerked his thumb between the two women. "This one's saying the other one saw a woman here this morning."

They'd already questioned one of the women, who was a maid at the motel, but hadn't seen the second woman yet.

"Espera." Cole sliced his hand through the air. "Wait. *Habla inglés, señora?"*

"Sí, yes, I speak English."

"What were you doing at the motel this morning?"

"Trabajo. I work here as a maid. I have the overnight shift."

"What time was this?"

"After seven o'clock, *señor.* I was almost done with work."

"Where did you see this woman? What did she look like?"

"By this car. I thought maybe she came out of the room. She walked past the car and she was pulling a suitcase." She twirled her finger in the air. "One with wheels."

"Did you see what she looked like?"

The maid put her hands about six inches apart. *"Flaca.* Skinny. Not tall, not short. She was wearing dark pants, maybe jeans, and a dark jacket."

The woman was observant. "Hair?"

"No, *señor."* She shook her head.

His brows shot up. "No hair?"

"Under a hat." She put her hands on top of her head. "Like *una...gorra*."

The other maid spoke up. "Like a knit beanie, pulled over her head."

Cole's pulse ratcheted up a notch. Like she was trying to disguise herself. "Did you get a good look at her face?"

"No, sorry. I notice because there was nobody else outside. I don't think she saw me. She walked past the car, fast, and then turned the corner up there." The maid pointed to the front of the motel.

"Toward the road." They'd already questioned the motel clerk and he hadn't seen or heard a thing. Had this mysterious woman poisoned Johnny Diamond, taken some of his cash and hightailed it out to the road to hitch a ride?

Cole got the contact information for the two women, thanked them and returned to the motel room, where the coroner had already loaded Diamond onto the gurney. The DEA and Cole personally had been trying to nail Diamond for four years. It figured that Diamond's death would provide even more questions than answers. Nothing had been easy with that guy.

What had Diamond been doing back in his old stomping grounds instead of plying his trade in Arizona, where he'd been wheeling and dealing for four years? Had that woman lured him this way?

Cole turned to Deputy Brookhurst. "Did you find any other fingerprints besides Diamond's in this room?"

"We barely found any of Diamond's."

Cole narrowed his eyes. "Wiped clean?"

"Looks like it."

"How about his phone? Did your guys search the Dumpsters and bushes for Diamond's phone? There's no way a man in Diamond's business would be without a cell."

"We looked. We'll try to track his number through the different providers and see if we can locate his phone by pinging." Brookhurst slapped Cole on the back. "Don't worry, Agent Pierson. We'll keep you guys in the loop. We called you as soon as we found out you had a flag on Johnny Diamond, didn't we?"

"You sure did, and I appreciate it. I've been after this SOB for a long time." Cole snapped his fingers. "Did any of the deputies do a search on the GPS in the stolen car? I noticed it had a built-in one."

"Damn, I don't think we've done that yet—a little distracted by what we found in the trunk."

"Yeah, poor Hazel McTavish. I wonder how she had the bad luck to run across Diamond." Cole flipped up the collar of his jacket. Seattle days could be cold enough, but Seattle nights could chill you down to your bones. "I'm going to check the GPS and see if I can find out where Diamond and his mysterious lady friend were headed."

He shouldered his way through the deputies and EMTs gathered around Hazel's trunk, and slid into the front seat of the car. He sniffed the air and got a whiff of some flowery scent—probably belonged to Hazel, but he'd have the King County boys dust for prints in here, too.

He poked his head out the door and yelled back, "I'm going to start the engine to look at the GPS."

The GPS beeped to life as he cranked on the ignition. With a gloved finger, he tapped the screen. He swiped his finger across Recent Destinations and blew out a breath—next stop Timberline, Washington.

HER HEART STUTTERED when the bell above the door of the tourist shop, Timberline Treasures, jingled. She turned from the bin she'd been filling with little stuffed frogs, and released a sigh.

She smiled at the family with two young kids. "Welcome. Let me know if you need anything."

The parents smiled back and started to browse through the key chains and magnets.

She wiped her sweaty palms on the seat of her jeans. She'd have to stop freaking out every time someone came into the store—or find another job. There was no way anyone could trace her to Timberline from that motel room. She'd wiped down all her prints and had even taken Larry's phone just in case he'd had any more information about her, or pictures, or any references to Timberline.

Not Larry, Johnny—Johnny Diamond. When she got to Timberline four days ago, one of her first stops had been the public library to use a computer. It hadn't taken her long to discover the dead man at the Stardust Motel was Johnny Diamond—drug dealer, thief and all-around bad guy.

What she'd been doing with him and how he'd wound

up dead, she still didn't have a clue. The online article she read didn't give a cause of death, but the authorities suspected homicide—no witnesses and no suspects.

She brushed a wisp of hair from her face. Diamond's phone didn't contain any incriminating evidence, and she'd destroyed and dumped it soon after.

Linda, her new boss, new best friend and owner of the store, came from the storage area in the back and plunked a box on the counter. "Can you help me sort through these items, Caroline?"

She'd adopted the name from the North Carolina plates of the semi that had picked her up a mile from that motel outside of Seattle. The choice of a last name had been trickier.

"Of course." She turned to the family. "Do you need any help?"

The mom swung a key chain around her finger. "We'll take one of these—just a little something with the town's name on it."

Caroline plunged her hand into a bin filled with furry frogs. Holding one up, she shook it. "How about one of these? It's a Pacific chorus frog and this particular toy is unique to Timberline."

The little girl's eyes widened as she tugged on her mom's sleeve. "Mom, can I have it?"

"Okay." She rolled her eyes at her husband, who shrugged.

Caroline brought the stuffed frog to the counter and winked at Linda. Linda rang up the family's purchases and when they left the store, she patted Caroline on the back. "You're a born salesperson."

Scooping the trinkets from the box, Caroline said, "I want to do my best to repay you for your kindness, Linda."

"When that haunted, hunted look leaves your eyes that will be repayment enough for me. It took my sister, Louise, years to recover from the abuse dished out by her boyfriend. When you told me your story of domestic violence and I saw that bruise under your eye—" she patted Caroline's hand "—I knew I had to help you."

Caroline blinked back tears as a pang of guilt twisted in her belly. She'd told Linda Gunderson a little lie to explain why she had no ID and why she was using a fake name, Caroline Johnson. She didn't want her abusive ex tracking her down.

Linda had gone above and beyond by introducing Caroline as her cousin's daughter, who'd moved out West for a fresh start. Linda extended her kindness even further by offering her the duplex next to her own, which she and her sister owned, and giving her a job at her shop so she could start earning some money with very few questions asked by the others in this small town.

But that haunted, hunted look in her eyes? That wouldn't go away until she knew her identity and what had happened at the Stardust Motel.

"I appreciate everything you've done for me, Linda."

"I needed help in the store, anyway, with Louise off on her cruise for a month." Linda sniffled and dabbed her nose. Then she shoved a handful of magnets at her. "Can you stock these and the pencils before you leave?"

"Of course." Caroline gathered the items and deposited them in their proper places around the store. When she was done, she took the empty box from the counter and left it by the back door of the storage room.

She lifted her black leather jacket and her new purse from the hook and returned to the store, where Linda was helping someone select a sweatshirt. Caroline waved on her way out.

If she hurried, she could make it to the library before it closed. She'd just scratched the surface of Johnny Diamond—enough to discover his talents for all forms of criminality, but not enough to find out about his personal life or any women in it. Had she been one of those women?

Once outside, she glanced at the moody sky, threatening rain, and then hurried across the street toward the civic center at the end of the block that boasted the sheriff's station, city hall and a cozy library.

She pushed through the glass doors and rounded the corner to the reference section. Two of the three public computers were occupied, but the third glowed in welcome and she strode toward it.

She was two steps away from pulling out the chair when a man slipped in front of her and plopped into it.

"Excuse me." She put her hands on her hips and hovered over his very broad shoulder. "I was just about to use this computer."

The man cranked his head over his shoulder and raised his eyebrows over a pair of greenish eyes. "I'm sorry. I was already seated here, but the log-in I got from the reference librarian didn't work and I went back for another."

"Oh." Caroline shifted her gaze to the pad of paper on the table next to the computer, which had been there before he grabbed the chair from under her nose. "I guess I'll wait."

"I really am sorry. I won't be long. The internet went out at my hotel. Otherwise, I'd be there on my laptop."

She waved her hand. "That's okay. Maybe one of the others will free up."

He turned his head to the side to take in the other two users, and his lips twisted into a smile. "Looks like they're here for the duration. I'll just be a few minutes."

"I'll be over by the magazines. Don't let anyone sneak in ahead of me."

"Wouldn't dream of it."

"Thanks." She pivoted toward a collection of love seats scattered in front of the magazine rack. He must have thought she was a real pain—or worse, that she'd been trying to come on to him. Attractive man like that probably had women making up all kinds of excuses to get close to him and exchange a few words.

She snatched a celebrity magazine encased in plastic from the rack and sat on the edge of one of the love seats, facing the computers.

True to his word, about five minutes later, the man stood up from the computer and stretched. He tapped on the keyboard and tucked his notebook under his arm.

She jumped to her feet. On her way back to the computer tables, she replaced the magazine. "That was fast."

"It's all yours. Have a nice evening."

"You, too." She settled in the chair, warm from his presence. She still had a password from the previous time she'd used the computers here, so she clicked a few keys and swore. The computer was locked and asking her for a password. The guy hadn't logged off.

She shrugged off her jacket and hung it on the back of the chair and tromped off to find the reference librarian.

The librarian looked up from her own computer behind the reference desk. "Can I help you?"

"I'm trying to use computer number one, but the person before me didn't log off and now I'm being prompted for a password that I don't have."

"That keeps happening. He probably did log off, but we've been having issues with that computer. If you don't mind, you can access with the same user log-in so we don't have to shut it down and restart it. The password is *timberline4,* the number, not the word. And it's all lowercase with no spaces."

"Thanks." Caroline returned to the computer and entered the password. As the computer digested her entry, she scooted her chair closer. She'd do another search on Johnny Diamond and try to dig a little deeper this time—beyond the article about his murder.

The computer monitor woke up, and she didn't even have to launch the search engine since the previous user hadn't closed out, thinking he'd logged off.

As the window filled the screen, an icy fear gripped her heart. She didn't have to search for Johnny Diamond—the man sitting here before had already done so.

Chapter Three

With her hands shaking and her belly in knots, Caroline scrolled through the display. Specifically, the man before her had done a search of Diamond's social media sites.

Did drug dealers really post pictures of their meals and funny cat videos? She clicked on the same links he'd accessed, but found nothing. No wonder he hadn't spent much time at the computer. Diamond didn't seem to have a social media footprint.

But why was that guy even checking? What was Diamond to him? She slumped in her chair and closed her eyes. He didn't look like an associate or fellow drug dealer. Too clean-cut for that, but what did she know?

Too clean-cut. She gripped the arms of the chair. A cop?

She forced herself to breathe. There was no way the cops could've traced her here. She'd hitched different rides to get to Timberline, avoiding bus stations and cameras.

Her fingers dug into the fabric on the arms of the chair. Unless the cops knew something about Diamond's destination. Her search of his background hadn't turned up anything on Timberline, so what connection could he have to this town except through her?

What connection did she have to this town? Why had she scrawled its name on a piece of paper and slipped it into the pocket of her jacket?

Her nose stung with tears as she pushed away from the table. She'd been a fool to come here. Nobody had recognized her yet or provided her with an identity, and she might've walked right into a trap set by Johnny Diamond and his cronies. The man using the computer could be one of those cronies. There must be plenty of clean-cut, attractive drug dealers out there. She'd have to leave this town.

Then what? She had no place else to go. Maybe she should just turn herself in. Could she really be charged with murder if she had no memory of the act? If she had no memory of her life?

She hadn't discovered much more about herself other than she knew Spanish. She'd come across a Spanish-language TV show and could understand every word they were saying. With her pale skin and light brown hair she didn't look Latina, but she could be half or have spent time in a foreign country. The possibilities were endless.

Blowing out a breath, she did a hard shutdown of the computer, just in case it didn't log her out, either. She didn't need anyone snooping into her browsing history, and Mr. Clean-cut would probably be none too happy if he found out someone had been snooping into his.

Maybe he was just interested in the murder. He didn't seem to recognize or have any interest in her.

She looped her purse across her body and squared her shoulders. She wasn't going to run. She had some digging to do first.

Ten minutes later she was seated at the bar of Sutter's, a local restaurant, flipping open a menu. She'd used the money from Diamond's bag—the drug money—to buy a few clothes, a purse, and pay first month's rent to Linda for the duplex. Once she got her life back, she'd return all the money she'd used to the police...anonymously.

The bartender tossed a cocktail napkin on the bar in front of her. "Are you ordering dinner?"

"I'll have the Sutter's burger and a root beer."

He took the menu from her and tapped it on the edge of the bar. "Caroline, right?"

"Good memory." *Unlike some people*.

"Part of my job. I'm Bud."

"I'll take that menu, Bud."

Caroline jerked her head to the side and almost slid off the bar stool.

The man from the library straddled his stool and took the menu from the bartender. He nodded at Caroline. "Were you able to get your work done on that computer? I think the library needs to upgrade."

"I—I was just—" she zeroed in on the menu "—looking up restaurants."

His green eyes flickered. "And you found this one."

He must've heard Bud say her name. She twisted the napkin in her lap. "Oh, I've been here before. I was checking out a few other places."

"Are you new to Timberline?"

"Sort of. My mother's cousin lives here and invited me out." She said a silent prayer for Linda Gunderson.

"Working at Evergreen Software like everyone else?"

Bud delivered her root beer with a wink, and she plunged her straw into the foam while he took the man's order, giving her time to think.

If she refused to answer his questions, it might seem suspicious, but she didn't want to tell him her life story—especially since she didn't have one, outside of waking up with a dead Johnny Diamond on a hotel room floor.

And she didn't want anyone to know *that* story.

He handed the menu to Bud and turned his rather sharp green eyes back to her. "Evergreen?"

"No. I'm working at my cousin's shop right now." She toyed with her straw. Two could play at this game. "I guess you're not a local, either, since you mentioned the internet connection in your hotel going down."

"That's right." He thanked Bud for his beer and took a sip through the foamy head. "I'm here doing some research for a book."

She released the breath she'd been holding in one slow exhale from parted lips. "What kind of book?"

"Sort of a travel book that also touches on the history of the area and local legends and customs." He held out his hand. "I'm Cole Pierson, by the way."

"Caroline Johnson." She wiped her fingers on her cocktail napkin and squeezed and released his hand quickly.

If Johnny Diamond was from this area, the book might explain why Cole was snooping around his social media. Maybe she could even get some info out of Cole about Diamond without arousing his suspicion.

The bartender delivered her food, and she hesitated.

Cole said, "Go ahead. You don't need to wait for me."

As she sawed her burger in half, Cole watched her with his head to one side. "Who's your cousin?"

Biting her lip, she placed her knife across the edge of her plate. Did his research make him naturally nosy, or did he sense her secrets?

"Linda Gunderson. She owns—"

"Timberline Treasures." His cell phone buzzed in his front shirt pocket, but he ignored it. "I heard about the store that Linda and her sister own. Maybe you can put in a good word for me so I can interview them."

"Louise is out of town, but I'm sure Linda would be happy to talk to you about Timberline's history, and you won't need an introduction from me."

"Is that a no?"

Bud placed a plate overflowing with mashed potatoes and several slices of meat loaf in front of Cole, and Cole whistled. "Looks good."

Caroline took a big bite of her burger. Did he expect her to respond? He really didn't need an introduction to Linda, since she loved talking about Timberline. Was he trying to extend their contact with each other?

Not that she minded, since he was a sweet piece of eye candy, but she had other priorities here.

He wiped his mouth with a napkin. "So how about it? You'll tell your cousin she can trust me?"

Caroline's heart skipped a beat. Trust him? How had they jumped from exchanging a few words over dinner to trust?

"Trust you?" She gave a nervous giggle. "I barely

know you. Like I said, you don't need an introduction from me. Linda will talk to you about Timberline."

He took another sip of beer and then picked up his knife and fork, holding them poised above his plate. "Do you know anything about Timberline? Did you visit your aunt much?"

"Cousin, and no. This is my first time out here."

He raised his brows as he cut into his meat loaf. "What brings you out here now?"

"Fresh start." She shrugged.

His glance shifted to her right cheek and the bruise she'd been masking with makeup. Or had she imagined that glance?

The man made her nervous. He asked too many questions. Everyone else had accepted her story without blinking an eye.

Time to deflect and go on the offensive.

"Is that what you were doing in the library? Research?"

"Looking into some local stories, local personalities."

She pushed away her half-eaten burger. Was Johnny Diamond a Timberline local? Maybe they'd been headed here together? If so, nobody seemed to recognize her yet.

"Why this town? What's so special about Timberline?" She needed an answer to that question herself. Why was the name of this town scribbled on a piece of paper and stuffed in her jacket pocket?

Cole cocked his head. "The Timberline Trio case for starters, and all the recent fall-out from that old case."

She nodded. She'd heard the Timberline Trio case mentioned a few times since she'd arrived, but didn't know much about it—something about some kidnappings that happened twenty-five years ago.

"You really haven't been around much, have you?"

"Well, I guess I won't be a good person for you to interview, then." She grabbed her check from the bar and plucked a ten and a five from her wallet. "Good luck with your research."

She slapped the check and the cash on the bar and spun around on the stool and hopped off. She couldn't get out of here fast enough.

"Nice meeting you, Caroline Johnson." His voice trailed behind her, but she didn't turn around.

Just because a stranger asked questions didn't mean you had to answer them—no matter how attractive the stranger was.

When she hit the sidewalk, she blew out a breath, which turned frosty in the night air.

Linda's duplex sat at the end of the main street in town, so Caroline was able to walk everywhere—at least to work and back. She had enough money from Johnny Diamond's loot to pay cash for a used car, but she didn't have a driver's license or any other ID. Walking would have to do for now.

She reached into her jacket pocket for her hat and tripped to a stop on the sidewalk. It must've fallen out. She scanned the ground around her, and then kicked at the curb with the toe of her boot.

She'd left it, along with her umbrella, on the bar, and

the last thing she wanted to do was go back in there and have another exchange with the nosy, if hunky, writer.

She could leave them at Sutter's and pick them up tomorrow. Nobody would steal a hat or umbrella. Bud had probably already put her things behind the bar.

Hugging her jacket around her body, she took a step, and a drop of rain pelted her cheek. She looked up at the dark sky and shivered. A ten-minute walk in the cold rain without a hat or umbrella would turn to misery after about one minute.

She had every right to march back into Sutter's and grab her hat and umbrella. She peeked through the window at Cole chatting with Bud. He was probably giving him the third degree, too.

She could always swing through the back entrance and maybe get one of the waitresses to get them for her. She took off at a swift pace and slipped into the alley between two businesses a few doors down from Sutter's.

Trailing her hand along one wall, she strode to the back of the buildings and turned right.

A low light illuminated the red awning above Sutter's back door. She tugged at the handle and stepped into the warmth. Moving toward the buzz of the restaurant, she had a clear view of the bar, and it looked like Cole had left.

The door to the men's room swung open, almost hitting her, and she jumped back.

"Nothing yet."

The low timbre of Cole's voice stunned her, and she flattened herself against the wall and ducked behind a cigarette machine.

The bathroom door slammed shut, but Cole stayed put in the hallway and continued his conversation, his back toward her.

"I met a woman tonight who sort of fit the profile—slim, new to town, had a dark cap, too."

He paused, while Caroline's heart thumped in her chest so loudly she couldn't believe he didn't hear it.

"Naw, she's related to someone here in town and isn't Diamond's type—too pretty, too normal."

Caroline closed her eyes and ground her teeth as her stomach lurched. If she got sick here and now, it would be all over, and Cole would know she wasn't normal—not at all.

"I'll keep looking around—and not a word to the boss, Craig."

He ended the call and went back to the bar.

Caroline crept to the back door and stumbled outside.

She might not be who she claimed to be…but neither was Cole Pierson.

Chapter Four

Cole pocketed his phone and perched on the edge of the bar stool. "How much do I owe you, Bud?"

"Do you want another beer?"

"I'm good. Just the check." Cole fingered the soft, black stocking cap on the bar beside him. Caroline had left in such a hurry she'd forgotten her hat and umbrella.

Her attitude had set off alarm bells in his head. She'd been skittish, nervous. Hadn't liked his questions. Didn't seem to know much about the town where she had relatives. Why would a young, attractive woman come to a small town like Timberline to relocate when she'd never been here before?

She didn't seem too concerned about his possible interview with Linda Gunderson. He'd make sure to follow through on that.

When Bud dropped the check, he pointed to the cap. "Caroline leave her hat?"

"Her umbrella, too." Cole ducked beneath the bar and hooked a finger around the umbrella's wrist strap. "I can put it back here for her."

"You know what?" Cole balled the hat in his fist

and shoved it into the pocket of his down jacket. "I'm stopping by her cousin's shop tomorrow, anyway. I'll return them to her."

"It's on you, then." Bud swept up the check and cash. "Change?"

"Keep it." Cole shoved his money clip into his front pocket. "What do you know about Caroline?"

Bud winked. "Pretty gal, huh?"

Bud had just given Cole the angle to play. "Does she have a husband or boyfriend lurking around?"

"She's single. Came here to stay with Linda Gunderson, her cousin, but then you know that, since you're going to Timberline Treasures to return Caroline's stuff."

"You've never seen her out here before?"

"Nope, but I don't know Linda that well. She rarely comes in to Sutter's and never sits at the bar, although she's no stranger to a little vino now and then." Bud hunched forward. "I heard Caroline was running from some trouble."

"Oh yeah?" Cole's pulse ticked up along with his interest. "What kind of trouble."

"Man trouble." Bud tapped his temple. "Came to town sporting a shiner. The word is she's running from a bad relationship, so you might want to think twice before heading down that road with her. Jealous boyfriends and husbands just might get you killed."

"You got that right." Cole rapped on the bar. "Thanks for the tip."

When he stepped outside, Cole zipped up his jacket

against the cold. Was Caroline's jealous boyfriend Johnny Diamond? And had she taken care of the problem herself?

THE NEXT MORNING after breakfast at his hotel, Cole drove his rental into town. The internet connection had been back up, and he'd done a search of Caroline Johnson—perfect name to reveal nothing and everything. He'd run her name through the DEA database, too, but nothing clicked.

He pulled his car into one of the two public lots on Main Street. The small town of Timberline had done a good job preparing for the increased population and traffic from Evergreen Software, the company that had revitalized this former mining and lumber town.

He tucked Caroline's hat and umbrella under one arm as he made his way to Timberline Treasures. Taking a deep breath, he flung open the door and a little bell jingled his arrival.

He didn't know if Caroline would be working today or not. If not, he could always grill Linda Gunderson about her cousin. But he hoped Caroline would be here…because he wanted to see her again.

An older woman looked up from behind the counter. "Good morning. Let me know if you need any help."

"I do need some help, but I don't need a Timberline frog."

"Oh? What do you need?"

Caroline stepped out from the back of the shop. "Information."

"I'm glad I found you here." Cole held up the cap and umbrella. "You left these at Sutter's last night."

Caroline's eyes widened. "And—and you took them?"

"I knew I'd be dropping by Timberline Treasures today to talk to Ms. Gunderson, so I told Bud I'd bring them to you."

"Thanks." She didn't make a move toward the counter, so he weaved his way through the bins and shelves on the store's floor and placed them on top of the glass counter. Then he thrust out his hand toward Linda. "Ms. Gunderson? I'm Cole Pierson. I'm writing a book about Timberline."

Linda's pale skin flushed as she shook his hand. "Oh dear, not a book on the Timberline Trio case, I hope."

"Not at all. This is a travel book that includes some of the town's lore. The Timberline Trio will probably make a brief appearance, but the crime is not the focus."

"Good, because we had some problems when a TV show came here to film. Nothing but trouble." She pursed her lips.

"I met your cousin Caroline last night at Sutter's and she said you might be willing to talk to me about the old Timberline."

"I think I can do that." She fluffed her permed gray hair. "Is this going to be on camera?"

He held up his cell. "Just recorded on my phone, if that's okay."

"That's fine. I'd be happy to talk with you. Are you also interviewing some of the real old-timers and the Quileute out on the reservation?"

Cole smiled over gritted teeth and nodded. This pretense could turn into a full-time job. "On my list."

The door tinkled behind him, and he glanced over his shoulder at an elderly couple struggling to push a stroller through the door. Cole maneuvered through the shop's displays to grab the door for them and hold it open.

The woman said, "Thank you so much. Our daughter has us bring so many items for the baby it's like pushing a truck instead of a stroller."

Cole hunched forward and chucked the baby beneath his chubby chin. "Is this your grandson?"

"Our first." Grandpa beamed.

The baby grabbed Cole's finger and gurgled. "You're a strong little guy, aren't you? Little bruiser."

He straightened up and met Caroline's wide eyes. Her eyebrows were raised and her mouth was slightly open. Heat rushed to his cheeks and he cleared his throat. "Cute kid."

"You're back." Linda bustled toward the couple and cooed over the baby.

As she chattered with the grandparents, Cole returned to the counter. "I was hoping to chat with Linda in the store today, but if she's too busy maybe I can buy her lunch."

"We're not going to be that busy today—not with the rain gusting through." Caroline tapped her fingers on the glass top. "Do you have kids?"

"Me? No. That?" He jerked his thumb toward the baby Linda now had in her arms. "Just making the grandparents feel good."

Actually, that had been one of many disappointments from his failed marriage. The fact that he and Wendy didn't have children. Although, given how the marriage ended—badly—that was probably a good thing.

"Do you?"

"Do I what?" Her blue eyes narrowed in her usual suspicious manner.

"Have kids?"

"Oh, no."

"Did your husband come out here with you for that fresh start?"

"I'm not…married." Her brows collided over her nose.

"Sorry." He held up his hands. "You started it…the personal questions."

"Then I apologize. You just seemed like a natural with that baby."

The couple at the door called out, "Goodbye. Have a nice day."

Cole waved.

"Friends of yours?" he asked as Linda returned to the register.

"Their daughter and son-in-law moved to Timberline when she took a job with Evergreen. They're retired and have been coming for visits since little Aaron was born." Linda rubbed her hands together. "Now, where were we? Do you have questions about Timberline?"

"Is it okay if we do this now? I don't want to interrupt business for you."

She flicked her fingers in the air. "We won't be busy, and now I have Caroline to watch the store for me."

"Can I buy you coffee across the street at Uncommon Grounds?"

"I told him he could talk to you in the back, Linda."

Linda knitted her brows and her gaze darted between the two of them. "Are you worried about being in the store by yourself, Caroline? You've done it before. I think you can handle it."

Did Caroline have a problem with him talking to Linda alone? Cole pasted a smile on his face. "It's up to you. Thought I'd buy you a coffee for your trouble."

"It does sound nice and I haven't had mine yet this morning." She patted Caroline's arm. "We'll just be across the street. If something comes up, give me a holler."

"Of course, of course." Caroline's shoulders dropped. "I know how much you enjoy talking about Timberline's history."

Some weird undercurrent passed between the two women, like a force field excluding him, and a muscle ticked in his jaw as his senses picked up on it.

Linda gave Caroline's arm another pat and then smacked the counter with the flat of her hand, which broke the tension. "It's settled. Coffee it is."

"Enjoy yourselves." Caroline brushed her light brown hair from her face. "I'll hold down the fort."

Cole stopped at the door. "Do you want us to bring you back anything?"

"No, thanks. I'm good."

The door shut behind them and Caroline waited for the bells to fade before covering her face with her hands.

She'd be a lot better once Cole Pierson, or whatever

his name was, left Timberline. That pat on the arm from Linda reassured her that her so-called cousin wouldn't be spilling the beans about her to Cole.

Maybe this interview was just what she needed to get Cole off her back. If he couldn't shake Linda's story that she was a cousin from back East who was escaping a bad relationship, maybe he'd move on.

And she could get back to the business of finding out who she was and what she was doing with a lowlife like Johnny Diamond.

She had discovered that the body in the trunk of the car outside the motel room was Hazel McTavish, and most likely Diamond had murdered Hazel when he stole her car at the airport in Seattle. So how far-fetched was it to assume that Caroline was also one of Diamond's victims?

Except she'd had a packed bag with her in the motel room. If he'd carjacked Hazel at the airport, maybe she'd been at the airport, too.

She rubbed the back of her head, where a hard knot had formed in place of the bump. She needed to regain her memory. How did people do that without going to a hospital and getting involved with law enforcement and psychiatrists?

The door to the shop swung open, and Caroline jumped. Her grip on the edge of the counter tightened as she watched a single man stroll through the door, shaking out his umbrella.

She had an idea of what one of Johnny Diamond's cronies might look like, and it wasn't this guy, with his crisp khakis and belted raincoat. But that's what she'd thought about Cole Pierson, too, and he obviously had some involvement with Diamond if he was looking for her.

She forced a smile to her face. "Can I help you find something? All the wood carvings in the front are 50 percent off."

The man tilted his head, a puzzled look in his eyes. "I'm just looking around. It's been a long time since I've been to Timberline."

Either she was paranoid or she was giving off a weird vibe, because this guy was checking her out. Probably a little of both. She coughed. "Feel free to browse."

She dusted behind the counter while keeping an eye on the shopper. He picked up and discarded many items after studying them intently.

He finally picked up one of the stuffed frogs and shook it.

"That's unique to Timberline. A local artist makes those."

"I think I used to have one of these frogs." He tossed it in the air and caught it by one leg. "I'll take it."

"Do you have children?"

"A daughter." He brought the frog to the counter.

"I'm sure she'll like it." Caroline's blood thrummed in her veins as she rang up the man's purchase under his scrutiny. He was studying her like he'd been studying the trinkets in the shop. Maybe he was just an intense guy.

"Is she with you? Your daughter?"

"No, I'm on a…business trip."

She counted his change into the palm of his hand and shoved the plastic bag toward him. "Hope she likes it."

He walked toward the door slowly and then stopped with his hand on the knob. "Are you a local?"

Did she just have one of those faces that invited questions, or was this a small-town thing?

"No. I'm staying with my cousin, who owns this shop."

His shoulders drooped. "Ahh, well, thank you."

"Enjoy your stay."

When the door closed, she collapsed against the counter. Would she suspect every person who walked in here of having ulterior motives? Of course, as the saying went, sometimes they really *were* out to get you.

She'd been right to suspect Cole. He'd lied to her about being a writer. He was searching for Johnny Diamond's companion. He was searching for her.

Crossing her arms, she strolled to the front door and leaned her forehead against the cool glass. She couldn't see into Uncommon Grounds, the coffee shop where Cole had taken Linda to grill her. Caroline had to trust that Linda would keep her secrets—even the ones she didn't know about. If Linda told Cole that she didn't have a second cousin named Caroline and had never laid eyes on her before she'd discovered her crying in the alley behind her store, he'd have every reason to believe she was the mystery woman with Diamond. And she had to be a mystery to Cole or he would've recognized her.

But who was *he*? If he was Diamond's associate, he might be wondering about some missing drug money.

Did the police mention how much money was found in the hotel room? Surely not. How would Diamond's cohorts know whether or not she'd stolen any money?

They might want to find her for other reasons. Revenge? Information? Could Cole be a cop?

The door to the Uncommon Grounds opened, and Caroline jerked back as Linda appeared on the sidewalk with Cole behind her. They were both laughing. That didn't mean anything, though. Cole Pierson was a charmer. He had the good looks to beguile a woman of any age.

Hadn't he cast a spell on her? Caroline should've taken her burger to go last night and gotten the heck out of Sutter's. If she had, she wouldn't have overheard his conversation. Better to know your enemies and keep them close.

She could keep Cole close—no problem.

His question about children had troubled her. She'd never considered that she might have a husband and children somewhere. Didn't she owe it to them to turn herself in to the police? If she were missing, they'd be looking for her. Even if she didn't come from this area, she might be able to find out if they were.

Maybe she should start looking at missing persons reports from other states.

As Linda and Cole approached the shop, Caroline backed away from the door and grabbed her duster.

They were still laughing when they entered on a wet gust of wind that sent the bells into a frenzy.

"Looks cold out there."

"It's freezing." Linda held out a coffee cup. "Which is why we got you a latte."

"Thanks, Linda." Caroline took the cup from her.

"Thank Cole. It was his idea."

"Thanks, Cole." She raised the cup in his direction. "Did you get what you wanted?"

"I think so. Enough to settle a few questions and raise a few more, which is always a good start to, ah… research."

She took a sip of coffee, eyeing him over the rim of her cup. The man drove her crazy. Was he toying with her?

The pressure of Linda's hand against the small of her back nudged her toward the counter. "I gave Cole a long, boring history of this shop and a more interesting account of the local artists, including Scarlett Easton, who's quite famous for her modern art, although I prefer her landscapes."

Caroline released a few short breaths. Linda had kept mum about her sudden appearance in Timberline.

"I sold a Libby Love frog while you were out living it up at Uncommon Grounds."

"Wonderful. I was wondering if we'd do any business today with the rain coming down."

Caroline jerked her thumb over her shoulder. "Might be a good day to continue with that inventory."

"I am taking the hint." Cole grabbed a frog. "And to show my appreciation for your time, I'll buy a frog, too."

"I thought you didn't have children."

"I don't have any, but that doesn't mean there's not a kid or two in my life."

Linda rang him up and tucked the frog into a plastic bag. "Let me know if you need anything else, Cole, and do go talk to Evelyn Foster out on the reservation. She can tell you about all the Quileute legends and myths."

"I'll do that." He held up his hand. "Stay dry."

Linda went to the window and watched him walk away. "Nice man. Good-looking, isn't he?"

"Cut to the chase, Linda. Did he ask about me?"

"Nothing to worry about, Caroline. He didn't ask anything a man attracted to a woman wouldn't ask."

Her nostrils flared. "Attracted? What does that mean?"

"Don't worry. I told him a little about your past." She held her thumb and index finger about an inch apart. "Just so he knows you're not ready to jump into anything right now."

"What did you tell him?" Caroline pressed two fingers to her temple. "Y-you didn't reveal that I really wasn't your cousin and had just arrived in town, did you? I'm not sure I trust him. M-my ex could've sent him. He could be looking for me right now."

Linda cinched both her wrists with a surprisingly strong grip. "I promised to keep your secrets, Caroline, and I'm not going back on that just for a pair of twinkling green eyes and a set of broad shoulders."

"What exactly did you tell him?"

"I stuck to the story. My cousin's daughter contacted me a few weeks ago, was in a bad relationship, wanted a fresh start and asked to visit for a while—and you are that cousin." She cocked her head. "Besides, if your ex really did send Cole looking for you, wouldn't he already know what you looked like? You have nothing to fear from Cole—except his devastating charm."

Biting her lip, Caroline folded her hands around her coffee cup. Had his conversation with Linda convinced Cole that Caroline Johnson was not the woman he was looking for, despite the black beanie?

If not, she had a lot more than Cole's devastating charm to fear.

SINCE LINDA HAD a bridge game with friends that evening that entailed her to concoct some complicated dessert to outdo the other ladies, Caroline had convinced her to leave early and let her close up.

Only a handful of customers had come into the store, and no more suspicious characters. Cole Pierson was the only suspicious character she'd actually met. She doubted more were on the way. She could either leave Timberline and abandon any hope of ever discovering why she'd been headed here originally, or stick it out and convince Cole she really was Linda Gunderson's cousin, who had no connection to Johnny Diamond, his drugs or his money.

She traced the edge of the piece of paper in her pocket on which she'd written the name and number of a therapist in Port Angeles. She'd asked Linda for a recommendation with the excuse that she wanted to work through her issues associated with the domestic violence. Linda was more than happy to oblige.

A therapist would have that confidentiality thing. The therapist probably couldn't keep a confession of murder confidential, but Caroline didn't believe she'd murdered Johnny Diamond. Maybe she'd killed him in self-defense, but she had no intention of admitting that to… She took the slip of paper out of her pocket and read aloud, "Dr. Jules Shipman."

Caroline locked the front door and flipped Open to Closed. Then she dipped her hand in her other pocket and called Dr. Shipman on the prepaid phone she'd purchased a few days ago.

She left a message after the beep, giving as little information as possible. Time enough to get into all the gory details of her life once she was lying on Dr. Shipman's couch.

She transferred the money from the register to the safe and dropped the accounting slip on top of the bills. She flicked off the lights and reached for her beanie and umbrella.

She smoothed her fingers across the soft material of the knit cap. She'd been foolish to keep this hat. How had Cole known the woman with Diamond had a hat like this? Had Johnny told him? Had someone seen her at the Stardust?

She pulled it on her head and shoved out the back door. She could stop playing this cat-and-mouse game and ask him. As she yanked the door shut, she shivered.

What then? Would he kill her? Interrogate her? Arrest her? She didn't know which of those options would be the worst.

As she marched along the alleyway running behind the Main Street shops, a noise caught her attention. She glanced over her shoulder at a man unfurling an umbrella.

He looked up and she could make out the pale oval of his face, but not much more. As he turned, the wind caught the edge of his trench coat and Caroline gasped.

Was he the man from the store who'd bought the Libby Love frog? Had he been watching her? Waiting for her?

She splashed through a puddle as she turned the corner and made a beeline for the more populated Main Street. Nobody was walking on the rain-soaked sidewalks, but people were going in and out of the restaurants and hopping into their cars.

She headed for the lights and warmth of Sutter's. She'd pick up some dinner to take back to her duplex, and mull over what she planned to say to Dr. Shipman.

She ducked into Sutter's and pointed to the bar as the hostess approached her. "I'm getting it to go."

She walked up to the bar and her stomach sank as a tall, good-looking man flashed a grin at her.

"We gotta stop meeting like this."

She tipped her chin at his almost empty plate. "Meat loaf again?"

"What can I say?" He spread his hands. "I'm a sucker for a home-cooked meal, even when it's not at home."

She waved down Bud. "Can I get a grilled chicken sandwich to go, with a side of sweet potato fries?"

"Coming right up." He jerked his thumb at Cole. "Did this guy give you your hat and umbrella?"

"He did."

"I was going to hold them behind the bar for you, but he said he'd be seeing you today."

"Did you think I was trying to steal them?" Cole

crumpled his napkin and dropped it in his plate. "I don't think the hat would've fit."

"Just keeping you honest, man." Bud winked at Caroline and she gave him a weak smile.

Everyone seemed to think Cole Pierson was the greatest guy ever. What would they think if they knew what she knew? That he was a lying SOB and possible drug dealer…or undercover cop.

A burst of rain pelted the window next to the bar and Cole whistled. "I think it's going to get worse before it gets better."

"It's bad out there." She dug for some cash in her purse, so she could pay and be on her way as soon as Bud came up with her order.

"Linda told me you didn't have a car here yet and you walk all over town."

"It's not bad."

"Except on a night like this. Can I give you a lift to your place? Even though it's not far, you'll get drenched walking that half mile."

Her jaw tightened. "Linda told you where I live?"

"She mentioned it was lucky the other side of the duplex she and her sister own was empty when you came to town." He leaned in close, his lips brushing the wet strands of her hair. "I'm not trying to move in on you or anything. I know you've had a rough time of it."

She blinked against the tears pricking her eyes. Was he referring to the brawl she'd apparently had with Johnny Diamond in the hotel room, or her manufactured past with the abusive ex? Cole's soothing tone almost made her want to confess everything to him. Almost.

She squared her shoulders. "Linda gossips too much. I dumped a jerk—nothing I can't handle."

"Thatta girl." A wide grin claimed his face. "Don't let the bastards bring you down."

"Here's your change, Cole." Bud swept up Cole's plate. "Your food will be up in a minute, Caroline."

Cole pocketed his cash. "So, how about it? I'm parked right out front."

She wanted to tell him to take a hike, keep his questions to himself and mind his own business. But that would make him even more suspicious, and maybe Linda had convinced him that she was really her cousin in need of a fresh start.

"I'd love a ride, thanks. If it's not too inconvenient."

"No problem at all."

Bud returned with a bag hanging from his fingers, and then twisted his head around to look at the TV mounted above the bar. He called to the other bartender. "Denny, turn up the volume. It's a story on the Johnny Diamond murder."

A chill raced down Caroline's spine, but she kept motionless.

Cole tipped his head back to take in the TV monitor. "I heard about that—found the guy with drugs and a car with a dead body in the trunk."

Her dinner still dangled from Bud's fingertips and she wanted to scream at him.

Cole asked, "Was he a local boy?"

"Diamond? No, but he ran with a local motorcycle gang, the Lords of Chaos."

The sounds around Caroline receded and she felt

like she was spinning through a vacuum. Larry. LC, the tattoo on Johnny Diamond's neck, stood for Lords of Chaos. Timberline had been Johnny Diamond's destination, not hers. Or maybe it had been hers, too. Nobody seemed to recognize her here, nobody except Cole Pierson, and for him her identity was all speculation.

"Do you think he was on his way here when he was killed?"

Bud hunched his shoulders. "I don't know. I hope not. Timberline has had enough trouble with the Lords."

The story ended. Denny turned down the sound and Caroline could breathe again—almost. "My food?"

"Sorry." He placed the bag on the counter. "Napkins and utensils inside."

She handed him a twenty. "Thanks, keep it."

Cole rose from his stool before she did. "Ready?"

"Uh-huh." She looked at Bud's curious expression and said, "Cole's giving me a ride home in the rain."

"Good idea. Have a good night."

Caroline turned, hugging the bag to her chest. So now if Cole murdered her and dumped her body in the woods, someone would connect him to her disappearance—and she was only half kidding.

She preceded Cole through the restaurant in thoughtful silence. Was the revelation of Johnny Diamond's connection to a motorcycle gang news to Cole or was he a member, too? She could always check his body for tattoos—and she was only half kidding about that, too.

As he opened the door for her, she slid a glance at his hand and the wrist revealed when his sleeve rode up. No tattoos there and she hadn't noticed any on his neck.

He opened his umbrella. "Here, get under. I'm just one door down."

A small sedan flashed its lights and beeped once, and Cole held the umbrella over her head while she climbed into the car. When he slammed the door, she did a quick survey of the console and the backseat.

No weapons and no dead bodies. Things were looking up.

He opened the driver's side door and collapsed his umbrella. As he slid onto the seat, he tossed the soggy umbrella in the rear. "Whew. This is a deluge. Even with your umbrella, you would've been soaked to the bone."

"Yeah, thanks."

He started the car and then turned to look at her, studying her profile. "Glad to do it."

"Straight ahead." She pinned her hands between her bouncing knees.

"All the way at the end where the businesses stop?"

"Yes."

The car crawled through the flooded streets, and Cole hunched forward. "You'd think a town in Washington would do a better job of drainage."

"Timberline's old."

"The influx of money from Evergreen Software should start going toward the town's infrastructure."

"Linda says it's helped a lot." Caroline tapped on the window. "Up ahead on the right where the two yellow lights are."

Cole pulled into the driveway she didn't use. "I'll get the door for you."

He pulled his umbrella from the backseat and unfurled it before getting out of the car. Two seconds later, he was opening her door, holding the umbrella over her head at great expense to his own well-being.

As she groped for the keys in her purse, he stayed right by her side, keeping her dry. When she made it to the covered porch, she pulled him up next to her. "You're drenched."

"You're not."

She released his sleeve. Was this his strategy? Cozy up to her so she'd spill her guts?

"Well, now it's all yours." She inserted her key into the lock and turned. "Thanks again and good luck with your book."

"Good luck to you, too, Caroline Johnson."

His voice trailed to a whisper as he melted back into the rain.

She blew out a breath and pushed open her door. That sounded like a goodbye. Linda must've been convincing.

She stepped into the small living room and the hair on the back of her neck quivered. Her gaze darted from the bookshelves to the pillows on the couch to the magazines stacked on the coffee table.

Someone had been in her house. A primal fear seized her and she turned and fled back into the driving rain.

Chapter Five

Cole dumped his umbrella in the backseat and slicked back his wet hair. He'd have to look elsewhere for Johnny Diamond's killer. One of the Realtors in town had mentioned a new single female renter at one of the cabins.

He took one last look at Caroline's door. He was relieved she wasn't connected to Diamond, but disappointed that he didn't need to spend any more time with her.

She sure as hell didn't want to spend any more time with him. After her experience with her husband, she must hate all men. He could understand that, but hell, he didn't hate all women after his own experience. But then his wife had just cheated on him, not given him a shiner.

A yellow oblong appeared on the porch and it took him a minute to realize that Caroline had opened the door. Had she changed her mind about him and wanted to invite him in for a drink? A guy could hope for the best.

As he squinted into the darkness, she flew off the porch and disappeared. Had she fallen?

He opened his door and peered through the sheets of rain at Caroline scrambling in the mud on the side of the short walkway to the porch, which she'd obviously missed.

"Caroline?" He slammed the car door and jogged toward her, leaving the umbrella behind in the car.

She looked up at him, her face pale, her eyes huge.

"What happened? What's wrong?" He crouched beside her and hooked his hands beneath her arms, pulling her up.

She stuttered through chattering teeth. "Someone… s-someone was in my h-house."

A shot of adrenaline coursed through Cole's body. "Someone's there now?"

"I—I don't know."

He pulled her onto the porch. "Stay here."

His hand hovering over the gun in his jacket pocket, he crept into the house. He blinked. It didn't look like there was a thing out of place. He'd expected chaos.

He moved silently across the wood floor, leaving a trail of puddles in his wake. He poked his head into the kitchen in case someone was crouched behind the counter that separated kitchen from living room. He couldn't detect any disturbance in this room, either.

He edged down the hallway and checked both bedrooms, including beneath the beds and in the closets, and even swept aside the shower curtain.

What had given Caroline the idea that someone had broken into her place? All the doors and windows were intact.

He zipped his pocket over his gun and returned to the porch, where Caroline was hugging the wall. "It's okay. There's nobody here."

He put his arm across her shoulders and felt the vibrations from her trembling body. He nudged her into the house and shut the door behind them.

"Can I get you something? Hot tea? A shot of whiskey? Both? You're wet and muddy."

She stared at him with wide eyes, her arms folded across her stomach. Her voice came out as a harsh whisper. "Was it you?"

Her soft words punched him in the gut. "Me? What?"

"Did you break in here to search through my things? To frighten me? To…to—" she waved her arm up and down his body "—to do this?"

"I don't understand." He stepped back. "Do you think I'm working for your husband or something?"

"I don't know."

"I'm not. I'm…not." He couldn't tell her about his mission here. He was doing this investigation on his own dime, anyway. He just wanted to reassure her. He wanted to snap his fingers and dissolve the fear that rimmed her eyes.

"I swear I don't know your husband, but from what Linda told me he sounds like a jerk. Look…" Cole ran a hand through his damp hair. "My stepdad used to knock my mom around. I'd never help out anyone who hurt women or children. Never."

Caroline's mouth softened and her lashes fluttered. "I'm sorry."

"You don't have to be. Just know I'm not on your husband's side. I don't even know your husband and wouldn't want to, except to plant one on his face."

She pulled her shoulders back. "Okay. It wasn't you."

"Of course not." Cranking his head from one side to the other, Cole asked, "How'd you know someone had been in here? Looks neat to me."

"I'm very particular. I can tell."

"Maybe Linda came over. She lives in the duplex next door, right? Maybe she had to get something or was going to leave something for you?"

Caroline shook her head and the droplets from her hair rained down on the floor. "Linda wouldn't do that. Someone was in here."

"And you think it was your ex or someone he sent?"

Her gaze dropped to her fingers, twisting in front of her. "Maybe. I suppose it could be a thief."

"A very neat thief."

"A thief who didn't want to be discovered."

"But one totally unaware of your super detection abilities." Cole smiled like an idiot, wanting to touch her, but afraid he'd send her over the edge. "You need to get out of those wet clothes. And the mud. You should see the mud."

"I dropped my dinner just inside the front door. I'm going to take a hot shower and curl up with my sweet potato fries."

"Do you want to call the police?"

"No!" A red tide washed over her cheeks beneath

the mud smears. "I have no proof anyone was here. The sheriff's department would put me down as a lunatic."

"Are you sure you're going to be okay here by yourself?"

"I'll be fine. Linda should be home soon. I'll ask her if she was here. Maybe you're right."

"I can stay while you shower. I mean, wait in here."

"Really, I'm okay. I've been on edge." She breezed past him and picked up the bag of food on the floor, and then opened the front door. "Thanks for coming back and helping me. I feel like a fool."

"I wasn't going to leave you flailing around in the mud."

She rolled her eyes. "That bad, huh?"

"You were scared and had a fall." He put his finger to his lips. "I won't tell a soul."

"Good night, Cole."

"Good night, Caroline." He left the house and waited on the porch as he listened for the click of the dead bolt.

Jamming his hands in his pockets, he put his head down and walked briskly to his car, keeping to the paved walkway.

He started the engine and cranked on the heat and defroster full blast. Blowing on his hands and rubbing them together, he eyed Caroline's duplex over the steering wheel.

Had he miscalculated? Would her ex really travel across the country to stalk her, or more unbelievably, send someone else to do it? How had she been so sure someone had broken in? Was it paranoia or was she really expecting trouble? And from what quarter? An abusive ex-husband, or from someone equally as dangerous? A drug trafficker looking for his money?

Cole felt a stab of guilt that he'd circled back to his original suspicions. He'd put those to rest after talking to Linda Gunderson, and what earthly reason would Linda have to lie for a complete stranger? To fabricate a whole life for this stranger?

Money? Timberline Treasures hardly looked like a bustling, profitable enterprise.

He threw the rental into gear and backed out of the driveway. Maybe Caroline had paid Linda to claim her as a cousin. Linda told a mighty convincing story.

As he watched Caroline's porchlight fade into the darkness in his rearview mirror, he set his jaw. There were too many puzzle pieces that didn't fit. Caroline Johnson hadn't quite convinced him that she wasn't the woman with Johnny Diamond.

Which meant…he wasn't done with her yet.

THE FOLLOWING MORNING, Caroline hunched over her coffee cup, trying to wake up. She'd waylaid Linda last night on her way in from her bridge party, but Linda insisted she hadn't let herself into Caroline's duplex.

Could she have imagined it? She shifted her gaze to the magazines stacked on the coffee table and the throw pillows set at a precise angle on the sofa. Ever alert, Caroline had set up the room so that any disruption could be detected—and she'd detected several. The edges of the magazines hadn't been lined up. One of the pillows had been positioned so that the tree on the front was upright, when she'd left it on its side.

If someone had broken in, at least he hadn't discovered her stash of money hidden under a loose floorboard in the bedroom closet. Was that what he'd been after?

She sipped her coffee and smacked the counter. How could she have been so stupid to display her fear in front of Cole?

At first he'd been solicitous, worried, had even revealed a piece of his own history, but she could see the doubt creeping back in his eyes the more she blabbed on about the break-in.

How ridiculous of her to admit that she was primed to recognize an intruder by the slightest hair out of place. And while she was sure there were a few exes who stalked their spouses after they'd moved from one coast to the other, how likely would it be for an abusive lover to sneak into his ex's house for a careful search? He'd be more apt to lie in wait and attack her, not rearrange her magazines.

Cole had to believe she was either crazy or lying, and she had her money on lying. He'd already suspected her of being the woman in the motel room with Diamond, and she'd just handed him further reason to investigate that suspicion.

And who the hell was Cole Pierson, anyway? She'd had no time to do an internet search on him, but she doubted she'd find any more on him than he'd found on her.

Her phone buzzed and she recognized the number as Dr. Shipman's. This could be the solution to all her problems—or just the beginning.

"Hello?"

"Is this Caroline Johnson?"

"It is."

"Hi, Caroline, this is Dr. Shipman returning your call."

"Yes, hello. Thank you." She moved to the sofa and sank against the cushions. "I was wondering if you could take on another patient. I'm interested in starting this week if you can fit me in."

"I am accepting new patients. You're in Timberline?"

"Yes."

"I had a cancellation this afternoon if you can manage to get here by two o'clock?"

She was working only until noon today and Linda had already told her she could borrow her car for appointments. "I can be there by two."

"Do you have medical-insurance coverage?"

"I—I'm paying cash. How much do you charge?"

"Seventy-five an hour, but we can work out a plan if that's too steep."

"I can manage that, thanks. I'll see you at two o'clock."

She collapsed against the tree cushion that had caused her such panic last night. Maybe Dr. Shipman could do hypnosis or something. She had to get her life back—whatever that life was.

Then she could stand tall before Cole and tell him the truth—or run and hide forever.

When she heard Linda's familiar tap at the door, Caroline pushed up from the sofa and stuffed her stocking feet in her ankle boots. She drew back the curtain and waved at Linda on the porch. Then she retrieved her purse from the kitchen counter and answered the door.

"Looks like we have a reprieve from the rain today." Caroline held out her hand, palm up, and caught a drop of water from the rain gutter.

"Would be nice to have a day to dry out." Linda tipped her head to the side. "Are you okay this morning?"

"I'm fine. I think I overreacted. Larry has no way of knowing I'm in Timberline or even Washington." She'd given her abusive ex-husband the first name she could think of.

"Totally understandable. My sister thought every bald guy she saw was her ex." Linda jingled her car keys. "Time to open the shop."

A feather of uneasiness tickled the back of Caroline's neck as she followed Linda to the car. "Speaking of bald guys, the man who bought the stuffed frog yesterday had a shaved head, said he used to live here and was back on business. Ring a bell with you?"

"Haven't heard about any returnees. Why do you ask?"

"I don't know. He seemed…" She shook her head. "I really don't know, Linda. I'm letting my imagination run wild."

As Linda settled into the driver's seat, she said, "You don't have to worry about that nice and very good-looking Cole Pierson. He's definitely here to write that book and his only interest in you is romantic."

Linda had no idea who Cole was…and neither did Caroline, but she doubted he had romance on his mind when he looked at her—especially now that she'd revealed her hand.

"Well, I'm not ready for romance. Even so, I appreciate that you kept our little secret. If he found out I was a stranger to town, others would find out, and I'm still nervous about Larry tracking me down."

Backing out of the driveway, Linda traced the seam of her lips with a finger. "He won't get any more out of me."

Caroline had a feeling all Cole had to do was crook his little finger at Linda and she'd tell him everything.

As they worked side by side in the shop, Caroline told Linda about her appointment with Dr. Shipman that afternoon. "So, is it okay if I borrow your car? I should have it back by five o'clock."

"Of course. I think you're doing the right thing by talking to someone, and Dr. Jules Shipman comes highly recommended."

The phone rang and Linda answered it. While she was talking, the door swung open and Cole strode into the shop.

Caroline swallowed. She had some backtracking to do with him to regain his trust.

"I thought you'd never dry off after that soaking you got last night." She flashed a big smile.

His eyebrows jumped to his hairline. Had she poured it on too thick?

"I took a hot shower and then went down to the hotel bar for a whiskey. Warmed me right up. How about you? Feeling better?"

"Yes." She covered her face with both hands. "I am

so sorry I went cray cray on you. I've been so stressed and on edge."

"So you don't think anyone broke into your place and searched it, including me?"

"Did I really accuse you?" She peeked through her fingers. "I'm an idiot. Nobody broke in. If my ex really wanted to contact me, he'd come here himself and confront me. That's more his style, anyway, but he's not going to do that. I never talked to him about my mother's family and he's never heard of Timberline."

"Glad to hear it and glad you're feeling better. I just came by to check on you."

Linda ended her call. "Good morning, Cole."

"As long as that rain stays away for a few more hours, it will be."

"Caroline." Linda turned to her. "I don't think I can loan you my car to go to Port Angeles, after all."

"Oh?" Caroline curled her hands into fists. Why did Linda have to talk about her personal business in front of Cole? Of course, Linda still believed he was a mild-mannered writer and didn't know he was some imposter looking for Johnny Diamond's last companion.

"That was my mechanic, Louie. He finally got a part for my car that's taken over a week to get here, and he wants to do the work this afternoon."

"Port Angeles?" Cole shoved a hand in the pocket of his jeans. "I was planning to go out there this morning."

Of course you were.

Caroline tucked her hair behind one ear. "My appointment isn't until this afternoon, but I appreciate the offer. And don't worry about the car, Linda. I'll reschedule the appointment."

Cole interrupted. "I can wait until this afternoon. I was just going to go to the library, since it's bigger than Timberline's and it has a couple of articles on microfiche that haven't been transferred online yet. It's no problem at all."

"Perfect." Linda clapped her hands together. "I don't want you to cancel your appointment, Caroline. Maybe you two can even stop for some lunch. You can leave before noon."

Linda was playing matchmaker. Cole had done such a number on her.

Caroline didn't want to be in Cole's presence any longer than she had to, especially trapped in a car with him. But if she refused, would that make her look suspicious again?

"I—I don't need lunch. I brought half of my sandwich from last night's dinner."

"We can skip lunch, but I'd be more than happy to drive you to Port Angeles. How long is your appointment?"

"About an hour."

"That works for me…unless you still think I'm the one who broke into your place last night."

"Caroline, did you really think that?" Linda's eyes grew round.

Great, now she seemed like the crazy one, and she'd seem even crazier if she refused a perfectly good ride from a perfectly respectable man like Cole. What possible excuse did she have?

"That was just me freaking out a little. I'd be happy to hitch a ride as long as I'm not putting you out."

"Then it's settled. I'll swing back around at twelve."

She waved as he left the store and then rounded on Linda. "Are you trying to set us up or something?"

"Was I that obvious?"

"Linda, I meant it. I'm really not interested in any romantic entanglements right now. I—I need to figure out why I put up with Larry's abuse in the first place before I can move on."

With tears in her eyes, Linda patted her back. "I know, dear. It would be nice to see you with a good man, and Cole Pierson is a good man."

A good liar.

Caroline hugged the older woman. "I appreciate your concern. I'm sure Cole has a million women vying for his attention back home—wherever that is. Did he ever tell you where he was from?"

"He lives in San Diego with a dog named Thor, and his sister watches the dog when he's on his travels."

Seemed Cole had concocted a more thorough backstory than she had.

The rest of the morning flew by and twelve o'clock arrived sooner than she wanted. Cole walked in on the dot.

"Are you ready?"

"In a minute. You're sure it's no trouble?"

"I need to get to Port Angeles myself. No trouble at all." He winked at Linda. "How about it, boss lady? Can your minion escape?"

"Of course. You two have fun."

Caroline rolled her eyes at Cole just so he'd know she wasn't hatching this plan with Linda, but maybe it wasn't such a bad idea for him to think she had the hots for him. That would really mess with his mind and distract him from whatever suspicions he already had about her.

"She means well." Cole opened the sedan door for her and shut it before she could respond. He slid onto the driver's seat. "Do you have an address in Port Angeles I can punch into the GPS?"

She plunged her hand into her purse and pulled out the slip of paper with Dr. Shipman's address. She read it off to Cole as he entered it into the car's GPS.

"Linda told me you're from San Diego. How long have you lived there?"

"All my life. Have you ever been there?"

"I..." She had no idea. "Visited once when I was a kid. How long have you been writing travel books?"

"This is my first try."

At least he wasn't going to try to lie his way through this part of his life. The rest was probably all fabricated, too. She'd keep peppering him with questions so he wouldn't have a chance to pin her down.

By the time they reached Port Angeles, she was exhausted from the effort. She'd kept him from needling beneath her exterior, though. He'd enjoyed talking about his big, slobbery dog so much she had to believe that part.

The voice on the GPS began directing them down streets, and he turned on the last one. "I'll just drop you off in front and pick you up in an hour?" He pulled up next to the curb in front of a two-story office building. "Do you want to take my cell number in case you're earlier or later?"

"Write it down." She shoved the piece of paper at him, not wanting him to see her prepaid phone and make any assumptions about it or her.

"Pen." He leaned across her lap to reach the glove compartment, and her hands hovered over his thick, sandy-colored hair. She had the strongest urge to run her fingers through it, but restrained herself.

He scribbled a number on the slip of paper and handed it back to her. "I'll be back in an hour, right here."

"Okay, thanks."

She waited until he drove away before heading toward the therapist's office. Cole hadn't asked her about the appointment and she hadn't volunteered.

Like everything she said to him, she had to consider the effect and consequences. She'd be relieved when he moved on—mostly. She'd miss seeing his familiar face around town. She'd either have to familiarize herself with a few more people in Timberline or get her memory back.

She walked beneath the stairs to Dr. Shipman's first-floor office, took a deep breath and opened the door, poking her head inside the reception area.

A potted plant waved in the corner and two chairs bracketed a small table sporting an open magazine.

Caroline crossed the room and pressed a red button with her thumb, following the instructions on the wall.

Then she turned and perched on the edge of one of

the chairs, clasping its arms. What would she discover about herself? It might be better to remain in blissful ignorance.

The door to the inner office opened, and Caroline jumped—her usual reaction to any sudden movement.

A woman stepped into the room with a slight curve to her lips and a soft twinkle in her dark eyes. "Caroline?"

"That's me." She bounded forward, her hand outstretched. "Thanks for seeing me on such short notice, Dr. Shipman."

"Call me Jules, and you did me a big favor by filling in for a cancellation today." She swung the door wide. "Come on in."

Caroline practically tiptoed into the room, with its muted light and comfortable furniture. She glanced from the chair to the sofa. "Where should I sit?"

"Wherever you like."

She took the sofa just in case she had to stretch out and have a good breakdown.

Jules sat in the armchair across from her. "Would you like some water? Coffee? Tea?"

"No, thank you."

Jules folded her hands in her lap with the same little smile on her face. "You can start. Tell me anything you have on your mind or why you're here today."

"Can I ask you a question first?"

"Of course."

"What I say in here—" Caroline circled her finger in the air "—to you, is confidential, isn't it? You won't tell anyone else. You won't tell the police."

The woman's expression didn't waver. "That's correct, unless you pose a danger to yourself or others."

She slumped against the back of the sofa. "I don't."

Jules settled into her own chair and took a sip of a fragrant tea…and waited.

Caroline rubbed her eyes. "I don't know who I am. I have amnesia."

Jules blinked. "How long have you been in this state?"

"Almost a week."

"Why don't you want to go to the police?"

Caroline sucked in her lower lip. If she told Dr. Shipman the truth, would she believe Caroline had killed Johnny Diamond? If so, that confidentiality thing would go right out the window. She'd have to play this by ear.

Leaning forward, she plucked a tissue from a box on the table next to the sofa. She dragged the tissue across her right cheekbone and pointed to the bruise healing there. "I have reason to believe I'm a victim of domestic violence."

"Do you also have a head injury? Something to explain the memory loss?"

"Yes." Caroline rubbed the bump on the back of her skull. "I'm afraid my spouse or partner will come after me. I—I think I'm on the run."

Jules steepled her fingertips together. "Is that why you asked about hypnosis in your message?"

"I'm hoping, through hypnosis, I can regain my memories."

"You didn't have a purse? ID?"

"Nothing. I've even checked a few missing-persons

websites. I just want to recover my identity and then I can figure out where I need to be."

"Why Timberline? Is that where you…woke up?"

"I regained consciousness in a park in Seattle. I had some cash in my jacket pocket and a scrap of paper with Timberline written on it, so I made my way there, thinking I had family or a lifeline there."

"Nothing?"

"I met a very kind stranger and she's been helping me, but I thought it was time to be proactive, since my memory doesn't seem to be returning on its own. I—I thought it might."

"It could, either in bits and pieces or prompted by trauma, but hopefully you won't have to experience any trauma to regain your memory." Dr. Shipman rose from her chair and stepped behind her desk. "Can we try something right now? I just want to see how susceptible you are."

Caroline's heart somersaulted in her chest. "Absolutely."

"I have a form for you to sign." Dr. Shipman pulled open a drawer and then looked up. "Is Caroline Johnson a made-up name?"

"Yes."

"Well, it's the only name you have, so you can sign as Caroline Johnson." She waved a piece of white paper at her.

When Dr. Shipman put the form in her hands, Caroline reviewed it quickly and scratched out the unfamiliar signature at the bottom. No warning listed on that piece of paper could be any worse than her current limbo hell.

"What now?" She settled back on the sofa, folding her hands in her lap.

"I have a pendant I use." Dr. Shipman opened her fist to reveal a silver disc on a chain. "It can be any object, but I like this one. Keep your eye on the disc. Relax, clear your mind, breathe deeply and don't concentrate on anything."

"If I can relax, it'll be a first time since this whole nightmare began."

"Which is perhaps why the memories haven't been forthcoming. When I snap my fingers and tell you to wake up, that will end the session." Dr. Shipman held up the pendant. "Open your mind. Let go. Shrug off the barriers."

Listening to Jules's soothing voice, Caroline focused on the disc shining in the dim room and tried to release every muscle group from head to toe. Her breathing deepened and her lashes fluttered as she fought to maintain a view of the gleaming circle that now represented a kind of lifeline.

The pendant faded. The room faded. Her body floated into the air.

A desert landscape, stark and rugged, invaded her head. People crowded against her, suffocating her, holding her in. She railed against them—her family. She had to get away from her family.

A woman's voice, soft and gentle, asked her questions, and she answered, because the woman wasn't one of her family members. She could talk to her even though she couldn't hear her questions, and couldn't hear her own answers to those questions.

Would the woman help her get away? She had to escape. She had to survive and return home. The desert? It was her home…and wasn't.

The sleepiness descended on her and her tongue felt too thick to form any more words. Would the nice lady leave her? Would she have to fight her way out on her own?

"Caroline."

The strange name floated into her consciousness. She didn't know a Caroline.

"Caroline? Wake up."

The voice sounded comforting, but it was meant for Caroline, not her.

"Caroline. Wake up."

A snapping sound jerked her out of her lethargy and into awareness. *Snap. Wake up.*

She passed a hand across her face and ran her tongue along her teeth. Caroline. *She* was Caroline. Her eyes flew open and she met Dr. Shipman's clear gaze. She floated back to the surface.

"How do you feel?"

"That depends. What happened?" Caroline clasped her hair into a ponytail. "I remember a desert, so different from the Washington landscape, and I'm pretty sure my real name isn't Caroline."

"When I asked where you were, you responded that you were home, but you didn't tell me where that was. You had family there, but you were trying to get away from them."

"Maybe—" Caroline touched her cheek "—this happened at home with my family. Maybe my spouse lives with my family and everyone wanted me to stay with him. I got the sense that I have a big family."

"Does that scenario feel right to you?" Dr. Shipman clenched her fist over her heart. "Here?"

"I knew the group of people in the desert. They had to be family. Maybe that's why they're not looking for me." Could Johnny Diamond have been a family member?

"Do you want to continue next week?"

"Absolutely." She smoothed her hands down the denim covering her thighs. "So, I'm susceptible to hypnosis and you think I can recover my memories?"

"I believe you can. In the meantime, do you feel safe?" Dr. Shipman rose from her chair as she pocketed the pendant. "That blank slate you face every day must be terrifying."

Caroline's mind flitted to the man coming to pick her up. She *did* feel safe with Cole, as long as she kept her identity a secret from him. He exuded a confidence and power that gave her a sense of security. Could you feel secure with someone who put you on edge all the time?

"Caroline? You *are* safe, aren't you?"

She pushed herself out of the comfy sofa. "I am— for now."

After paying Dr. Shipman in cash and setting up her next appointment, Caroline returned to the reception area. The outside door opened and she tripped to a stop.

A dark-skinned man with shaggy brown hair edged into the office, keeping his head down.

Caroline averted her gaze and strode past him and out the door. Everyone deserved their privacy.

She pulled the door shut behind her and peered down the street, looking both ways. She didn't want Cole to see her coming out of a therapist's office, although it would bolster her story. Why would Johnny Diamond's accomplice or murderer want to see a shrink?

In fact, her appointment with Dr. Shipman might be just the thing to get her off Cole's radar again.

Caroline blew out a breath and headed toward the sidewalk just as he pulled up to the curb across the street. Waving, she strode to the car and yanked open the passenger-side door.

She dropped onto the seat and swung her purse into the back. "How'd your research go?"

He nodded once. "Good. Everything okay with your…appointment?"

"You're very discreet, but I don't have any secrets." She smoothed her hair back from her face. "In case you haven't guessed, I just saw a therapist."

His head jerked up. "Really?"

"Linda thought it was a good idea, and after speaking with Dr. Shipman, I have to agree." Caroline's openness extended only so far. She didn't have to tell him about the hypnosis or what she'd discovered from it.

"That's great." He jerked his thumb over his shoulder as he pulled away. "Dr. Shipman's the therapist? I saw her name on the directory when I dropped you off."

"Yeah. I like her."

"Good. Have you ever been in an abusive relationship before?" He held up one hand. "And you can tell me to mind my own business."

She'd wanted to tell him to mind his own business

on several occasions, but this wasn't one of them. "That was my first and my last."

"Good to hear that. My mom didn't stay long with her abuser, either."

Caroline let him talk, sealing her lips, not wanting to get into any details about her relationship with Larry—details she might have to recall later.

Cole hit the steering wheel with the heel of his hand. "Let's celebrate your new resolve."

"Celebrate?"

"I know you ate lunch before we left, but I didn't. Do you want to get something to eat, or just a coffee, before we head back to Timberline?"

"Sure. I'd like that." And for a change with Cole, she was telling the truth. The therapy seemed to allay his suspicions again, and with Dr. Shipman's help she was on the road to recovering her memories. For the first time since she'd regained consciousness at the Stardust, Caroline had some hope.

As they drove toward the wharf, Cole turned his head to glance at her. "Restaurant or coffeehouse?"

"You're the one eating. You choose. I can have a coffee anywhere."

He pulled into a small parking lot of a café that sported a blue-and-white-striped awning over the front door. "Looks like I can get a sandwich here."

He stepped out of the car and slammed the door. As he came around to the passenger side, she cracked open the door.

Pointing into the car, he said, "I left my jacket in

the backseat. Can you grab it for me when you get your purse?"

"Okay." She twisted around and poked her head into the back. As she tugged his jacket from the seat, his wallet fell to the floor. Her fingertips tingled, and then she snatched the wallet and shoved it into her purse.

Curling her fingers around the strap of her bag, she straightened up and slid from the car. She pressed Cole's jacket into his arms. "Here you go."

"Thanks."

She held her breath. Would he notice his missing wallet right away?

He didn't even put on the jacket as he guided her into the restaurant, with his hand on her arm.

The waitress waved toward the back of the room. "Anywhere is fine."

They took a booth in the corner, and Cole plucked two menus from a holder on the edge of the table.

Caroline hugged her purse to her chest. "I'm going to use the ladies' room first. Order me a cappuccino if the waitress comes around."

With her heart pounding, she made a beeline for the restroom. She stepped into the single bathroom and locked the door behind her. Leaning against it, she closed her eyes and took a deep breath.

This was the second time in a week that she'd stolen from someone—not that she planned to steal anything from Cole. But she didn't want to let down her guard now that he seemed to trust her. She still had to pin down his true identity, as he'd tried to do with her.

With shaking hands, she unzipped her bag and

reached inside for Cole's wallet. She wedged her shoulder against the door and flipped open the leather.

Cole stared back at her from a California driver's license. Hadn't lied about being a California boy. Ignoring the cash in the billfold, she jammed her fingers into the slot behind his license and pulled out a stack of cards.

The gold-embossed letters on the top card blurred before her eyes and she slid down the length of the door until she was crouching against it.

Cole Pierson was a DEA agent, and he must be looking for the woman he believed had murdered Johnny Diamond and stolen his drug money.

Cole was looking for her.

Chapter Six

Cole ordered Caroline's coffee, and a sandwich and soda for himself. His cell phone rang from his jacket pocket and he grabbed the folds of leather, feeling for it. Then he reached for his other pocket and pulled his phone out.

He released a breath when he saw his sister's number pop up instead of the agency's. He didn't need his boss tracking him down right now. Only his partner, Craig Delgado, knew he was using his vacation time to follow up on Diamond's murder. Cole had worked too long and hard on the Diamond case to drop it now—even though his quarry was dead.

"Hey, Kristi. I can't talk right now. What's up?"

She snorted over the line. "Why are you asking me what's up in the same breath as telling me you can't talk?"

"Just being polite. I'm working right now."

"Okay. Just called to shoot the breeze. Give me a call back when you're not busy with important DEA stuff."

"Everything good?"

"I have a husband to worry about me now, big brother. Relax. Everything's fine."

"Then I'll call you later." He ended the call and dropped the phone back into his jacket pocket. Then he frowned and patted the other pocket.

Had he left his wallet at the sheriff's station? He picked up the jacket and looked at the seat. He even checked the inside breast pocket, which he never used.

He'd tossed his jacket into the backseat of his rental when he'd left the station, and he was positive his wallet had been in the pocket. It must've fallen out.

He glanced toward the restrooms and then flagged down the waitress. "I'm going back to my car for a minute. Can you let my friend know in case she gets back before I do?"

"Sure."

He stuffed his arms in his jacket sleeves and jogged out to the rental. He opened the back door and ducked inside the car, running his hands along the seat and peering beneath it.

Caroline's purse had been back here, too. She'd grabbed his jacket for him. What else had she grabbed? Did she still suspect him of being some crony of her husband's?

He slammed the door and leaned against the car with his arms crossed. What would she discover from his wallet? He'd left his badge in the hotel safe, but he had business cards in case he needed them for the various police agencies.

She'd find out he was a DEA agent…and that he'd been lying about it. So what?

The fact that Caroline would see him as a liar and an untrustworthy person burned a hole in his gut. She'd had enough people in her life she couldn't trust. He'd wanted to be different.

Cole shook his head. It didn't matter, did it? He'd exhaust his investigation in Timberline and then return to work—with or without Diamond's hotel companion—and Caroline would continue to pick up the pieces of her shattered life with her cousin in the small-town embrace of Timberline.

If they could enjoy each other's company for a week or so, maybe he could do a little to restore her faith in men. She would understand why he'd withheld the truth of his identity from her, just as he understood she'd felt compelled to lift his wallet to check him out.

With these noble thoughts, he pushed himself off the car and returned to the restaurant. As he walked through the door, Caroline's light-colored eyes watched him over the rim of her oversize coffee cup.

"Everything okay?"

He slid into the booth across from her. "I thought I forgot my wallet in the car."

"Oh." Her cheeks reddened as she reached for her purse. "I have it here."

His eyes narrowed as he watched her toss the wallet on the table between them and then slurp from her coffee cup.

"I—I didn't take your money." Glancing up, she covered her mouth with her hand and giggled.

He recognized that as a nervous response. "How did you happen to have it in your purse?"

"It fell from your pocket when I got your jacket out of the back, and I dropped it in my purse. It was easier than trying to stuff it back in your jacket." She blinked. "Sorry."

"Caroline." He took her hand in his and played with her fingers, warm from her coffee mug. "It's okay. You still suspected me of having some connection with… Larry, right? I can understand that you saw my wallet and decided to check things out for yourself."

"I… I—"

He put a finger to her plump lips to stop any more lies from escaping. "I'm not mad. I get it."

"I just… I'm sorry."

"And now you know I work for the Drug Enforcement Agency, and I'm not really writing a book." He squeezed and released her fingers before dragging a napkin into his lap.

"I did see that. I'm really sorry." Her mouth stretched into a tight grin. "Are you gonna have to kill me now?"

"Funny. Actually, I'm doing a little legwork on my own time."

"What does that mean? If you can tell me."

"Technically, I'm on vacation." He pulled some lettuce from his sandwich and dropped it on the plate.

"You have an interesting way of spending your time off."

"It's just that I've been tracking this one guy for a while. Lucky me, he wound up dead, but I still have unanswered questions about him and…his last days." Cole took a big bite of his sandwich to keep himself from divulging any more details to Caroline.

He'd come clean about his identity. He didn't have to reveal his whole case file on Johnny Diamond. She probably didn't care, anyway. Wendy had hated hearing about his work—had found it boring. Turned out she had more fun on the other side of the law.

Cole swallowed and took a long drink of soda.

"Drug dealers in Timberline?" Caroline widened her eyes. "Somehow I never expected that from this place."

"Really? You haven't been following the Timberline Trio case very closely, have you?"

"N-no."

"Turns out those three kids were kidnapped in exchange for some drugs."

"That's terrible. What happened to them—the kids, I mean?"

Cole cocked his head and squinted at her. "You really are out of the loop. Nobody knows. The kids vanished without a trace. The FBI with the help of some locals finally nailed down the who, but not the why or where."

"Who kidnapped them?"

"Some local biker gang kidnapped the kids for some sick dude who was part Quileute, the Native American tribe out here. That didn't sit well with the tribe members. If they ever got their hands on him, he'd be a goner, nothing left for the FBI to arrest."

"So, they don't know where he is?"

"He disappeared shortly after the kidnappings, but was never tied to the crimes until the Lords of Chaos became part of the picture. Nobody knows what he did with those kids, and their bodies were never found."

Caroline hunched her shoulders and took another sip of her cappuccino.

Way to win over and impress women. Wendy hadn't

appreciated his talk about work; why would Caroline? Especially since she'd so recently experienced violence in her own life.

"Sorry, too much information." Cole took another bite of his sandwich. Seemed to be the only way to shut himself up.

"It's sad and tragic, but it doesn't bother me to hear about it. No wonder Linda doesn't talk about the case."

"How's your cappuccino?"

"It's nice. How's your sandwich?"

He raised his eyes to the ceiling as she caught him in midbite.

"How long are you going to be investigating in Timberline and what exactly are you looking for?"

He chewed a little longer, searching for an answer. If he admitted that the possibility of finding Johnny Diamond's female companion and probable killer had drawn him here to Timberline, she'd figure out that's why he'd been stalking her. He might owe her the truth, but he didn't owe her an answer. He was still on DEA business even though the agency, outside of his partner, didn't have a clue he was here.

Cole wiped his mouth with his napkin. "Turns out my dead drug dealer was from around this area, or at least hung out with the local biker gang."

"I figured that." Caroline traced the edge of her cup with her fingertip. "And how much time are you going to give it?"

"Maybe a week. I have to return to my real job sometime." He drew a circle in the air above the remaining half of his sandwich. "Sure you're not hungry? Do you want this?"

"No, thanks, but does the sandwich offer mean you forgive me for lifting your wallet?" She covered her eyes with one hand. "I don't know what came over me."

"I get it, but I hope this conversation and my business cards put to rest the idea that I came out here to look for you."

A rush of pink washed across her cheeks. "That whole notion was silly."

"Don't worry about it. Looks like you're getting on the right track with the therapy and everything."

"I think she'll really help."

The waitress hovered at their table, waving the check. "Can I get you anything else?"

"I'm good." Cole raised his brows at Caroline, and she shook her head. "Just the check."

The woman set it on the table with a flourish.

"Let me get this." Caroline dragged her purse into her lap. "I still feel so guilty about snatching your wallet and violating your privacy."

"All you had was coffee."

Cole reached for his wallet, but she put her hand over his. "Let me get it."

"Okay, but it's not necessary to make it up to me."

"I insist." She plucked a twenty from her wallet and placed a saltshaker on top of it and the check.

They left the restaurant and Cole slung his jacket over his arm. Any trace of the sun had ducked behind some rolling gray clouds. He tipped his head back to look at the sky. "Rain again?"

"Seems to be a perpetual state of affairs up here. I prefer the dry heat of the desert."

Caroline tripped over a crack in the pavement, and Cole caught her arm. "Whoa."

She tucked her chin against her chest as she hunched into her jacket and broke away from him, rushing to the car as if she thought the skies would open up on them then and there.

As he opened the car door for her, Caroline's words sunk into his consciousness. "The desert? I thought you were from back East somewhere. And don't worry, I'm not going to ask you from where."

"I am, but that doesn't mean I don't like the desert climate. I'm sick of snow, and I'm getting pretty tired of the rain already."

"You and me both." He shut the door and made his way to the driver's side. He thought they'd gotten over the distrust, but she was still skittish. Must be habit. She'd probably walked on eggshells with that scumbag husband of hers.

Caroline was quiet, thoughtful, on the ride back to Timberline. Cole didn't want to disturb her train of thought. In fact, he didn't want to disturb her anymore.

She pushed all his buttons and he was attracted to her beyond belief, but her actions screamed of complications he didn't want or need right now. He could see pursuing a relationship with her once he'd wrapped up here if she'd been a Timberline local, someone with a life and a plan.

But Caroline seemed lost, rootless and afraid. He wanted to rescue her in the worst way, but he had other priorities right now. And it wasn't like she was crying out to be saved.

She had him at arm's length and wanted to keep him there.

As they drove into Timberline, he said, "I hope Linda got her car fixed."

"So do I. Thanks again for taking me into Port Angeles for my appointment."

He rolled up to the curb in front of Timberline Treasures. "No problem. I'm just going to stick my head in and say hello to Linda."

Caroline didn't tell him to stay in the car, but she didn't exactly encourage him, either. He thought they'd made some progress over lunch, but she'd done a one-eighty once they got to the car, and the ride home couldn't have been chillier if they'd been riding in a convertible in the rain.

He yanked the door of the shop open for her, feeling irritated with himself. He didn't need any more complicated women in his life—no matter how good she looked in her skinny jeans.

Linda glanced up from helping a customer and smiled.

She probably thought her little matchmaking scheme had come off famously. Cole would let Caroline break the bad news to her and tell her what had gone wrong, because he sure as hell didn't know.

Not wanting to get into any small talk with Cole, Caroline wandered around the shop, picking up and replacing items she saw a hundred times a day.

Where had her preference for the desert come from? The fact that she'd blurted it out to Cole had to mean her memory was coming back, unless she'd been influenced by the hypnosis. She'd have to watch what she said around the DEA agent.

DEA agent looking for a suspect in Johnny's murder was better than drug dealer looking for his missing cash, but only marginally. If he had any idea that she'd been the last person to see Diamond alive, even if she couldn't remember it, he'd haul her into custody so fast her head would spin.

The customer finally left the shop and Caroline asked, "Did you get your car fixed?"

"I did. Did you get to your appointment okay?" Linda glanced quickly at Cole.

"It's okay. Cole knows I was seeing a therapist."

"And I wholeheartedly approve—" he held up his hand "—not that Caroline needs approval from me."

"And you?" Linda hunched forward, folding her arms on the counter. "Did you find what you needed at the Port Angeles library?"

He slid a sideways glance at Caroline before answering. "Yep."

Cole hadn't asked her to keep quiet about his real purpose in Timberline, but who was she to spill anyone else's secrets?

"We even had a bite to eat before we hit the road back to Timberline," she said.

Linda's eyes sparkled. "Sounds like a nice day. I'm glad Cole could step in and give you a lift."

"It worked out." Caroline pressed her lips together.

She didn't want to give Linda any ideas about her and Cole. Even if she were in a position to start a relationship, it wouldn't be with a DEA agent.

"It's always nice getting to know someone." Linda beamed.

"We did get to know a little more about each other." Cole crossed his arms. "What I learned about Caroline is that she doesn't know much about her adopted home."

"Timberline?" Linda's smile froze on her face. "She never visited before, but she's learning something new every day."

Caroline nodded as her stomach sank. Linda needed to stop talking before she revealed too much information, and maybe she needed to leave town so she wouldn't be putting Linda in any more awkward situations where Linda had to lie—especially to DEA agents.

Dr. Shipman had indicated that hypnosis could work for her, so it could probably work for her anywhere and with anyone. She should try to recover her identity far, far away from Timberline—and Cole Pierson.

"She didn't even know that the biggest mystery out of Timberline, the kidnapping of those three children, had been partially solved. But I guess you had your own issues to deal with, didn't you, Caroline?"

Caroline ground her back teeth together. Did he suspect her again? He kept swinging back and forth between believing she was Linda's cousin looking for a fresh start and suspecting she might be the woman in Diamond's motel room at the time of his death.

"Yeah, I haven't been paying much attention to the local news."

Linda sighed. "I'm glad the authorities finally identified who took those kids. Now if someone could only figure out what Rocky did with them."

"Rocky?" Caroline stopped swinging the key chain around her finger as her heart skipped a beat. Rocky was the name on the text Johnny had gotten on his phone.

So she was connected not only to a drug dealer, but to a kidnapper. What kind of madness had she escaped?

Chapter Seven

"R-Rocky?" Caroline swayed on her feet and dropped the key chain back in the bin.

Linda responded in a hard voice. "Rocky Whitecotton. He was Quileute, although they've all but disowned him. One of their own, Scarlett Easton, made the connection between Rocky and the Timberline Trio, along with a former member of the Lords of Chaos."

Cole had moved closer to Caroline, almost hovering, but she didn't turn his way. What would he see in her face?

"Lords of Chaos?" She sounded like a parrot, but she couldn't form a coherent thought in her head.

"That motorcycle gang. I think I mentioned it to you before." Cole's voice sounded close, almost like a whisper in her ear, almost accusing.

She swallowed and scooped her hair back from her face. "Wow, Timberline does have quite a sordid history. Are you going to put all of this in your *book*, Cole?"

He jerked back sharply and sucked in a breath. "Not really the kind of thing my books focus on. I want to show the charm of a place, not unearth all of its dirty little secrets."

"Your *books*? I thought this was your first one."

"This one and the ones I plan to write in the future."

Linda had been glancing between the two of them with a crease between her brows. "Anyway, the FBI knows that Rocky was responsible for the kidnappings, that he gave the Lords of Chaos drugs to do the dirty work, but they don't know why he did it, or what he did with the children."

"I've heard all this before." Cole jerked his thumb over his shoulder. "I'm going to hit the road, but I think you left your phone in my car, Caroline. Do you want to come out with me to get it? Or I could drive you home."

"I'll do a little work here and go home with Linda, but I'll come get my phone." She patted her throwaway phone in the pocket of her jacket just to make sure it was there, and then followed Cole through the door.

Before he could open his mouth, she spun around on him. "Don't worry. I'm not going to tell Linda or anyone else that you're DEA. Did you think I would?"

"I didn't think so." He scratched the sexy stubble on his chin. "But for a minute in there, I thought you were going to blow my cover. I'm sorry I'm asking you to lie for me. I don't like that, but you did go snooping through my wallet. I just don't want the locals to know that I'm looking into Johnny Diamond's past."

"Maybe the good folks of Timberline would be able to help you. I doubt anyone here has any loyalty to some scumbag drug dealer who's connected to an outlaw biker gang."

"You never know about these small towns. I'm sure there are still a lot of people here who have connections to the Lords. A few of them were just in town last month, causing trouble, as usual."

"They were here? In Timberline?" Caroline crossed her arms over her stomach.

What did she think she'd find here? She'd discovered nothing about her identity, but had plenty of reason to regret her decision to come to Timberline. She should've stayed in Seattle, a big city where she could get lost. She could've found a hypnotherapist there, worked things out in relative safety and anonymity.

Of course, if she hadn't come to Timberline she never would've heard Rocky's name or found out that a DEA agent was hot on her heels.

She never would've met Cole at all.

He squeezed her shoulder. "Are you okay? It's not like the Lords are going to come after you or wreak havoc through Timberline."

No, just wreak havoc with her mind—like Cole was doing now with his comforting hand on her shoulder. Maybe she should confess everything to him. He'd want to know that Diamond had received a text mentioning Rocky. It couldn't be a coincidence. Rocky was not a common name. Did that mean that Diamond also had something to do with the Timberline Trio? Maybe his connection to Rocky could help the FBI find out what had happened to those kids twenty-five years ago. Didn't she owe it to them to speak up?

"I just hate the thought of violence. I really do. I

couldn't harm a spider—and I hate spiders. I don't understand people who commit violent acts."

Cole tilted his head to one side, studying her face. "Just keep seeing Dr. Shipman. I'm sure you'll work things out, Caroline."

She stiffened. That sounded like a goodbye. Maybe he didn't want anyone around him who knew his true business in Timberline. She bit the inside of her cheek to bring herself back to reality. This was what she wanted—get rid of Cole and his questioning eyes, his hovering presence, his suspicions.

"You're right. Once I get sorted out, I probably won't even stay here in Timberline. I'll most likely get lost in some big city."

"In the desert."

"What?" Her gaze flew to his face.

"You said you liked the desert. You could head to Phoenix or Albuquerque. Hell, even L.A.'s a desert."

"I might do that." She plucked her phone from her pocket. "I know I don't need my phone from your car, so thanks for the ride and…and say goodbye before you leave town."

"I will." His fingers brushed her cheek and he turned toward his car.

She didn't wait for him to drive off. She pivoted toward the store and shoved the door hard, setting off the tinkling of the bells.

"What happened? Didn't you two hit it off?" Linda screwed up her mouth. "I sensed a lot of tension between you."

"I appreciate your efforts, Linda, but I'm not ready for any romantic entanglements right now."

"But if you were—" Linda winked "—Cole would be just the man to start with. He's so…safe. A girl would feel protected with him."

Linda must be picking up on Cole's law enforcement vibe, just as Caroline had. As a DEA agent, he was accustomed to being large and in charge. He was even here in Timberline on his own time. He was obviously dedicated to his job and justice—and that would mean moving heaven and earth to find Diamond's accomplice.

Caroline could never tell him about her role in Johnny Diamond's life. He wouldn't understand. For all his smiling helpfulness, the man had a hard edge. She saw it in his eyes when he talked about the drug dealers and the kidnappers and the outlaw biker gang. He had little patience for people like that—people like her.

The lawman and the criminal—ha, that would never work in a million years.

"I'm sure he'll make some woman a great husband. He even likes babies."

"Just not you." Linda came from behind the counter and gave Caroline a hug. "How did your therapy go? Do you think it's going to help you? I really think it saved my sister."

"I think it will help." Deserts, large families and escape—it was a start.

LATER THAT EVENING, Linda was feeling social and invited Caroline out to dinner. Caroline wanted to stay away from Sutter's, since that seemed to be Cole's dining choice most evenings, but when Linda went out for dinner that's where she went.

A quick survey of the dining room assured Caroline that Cole had either chosen another place tonight or hadn't made it over here yet. She and Linda took a table in the middle of the room—another of Linda's conditions. She liked to see and be seen when she went out. She missed her sister more than she let on.

Caroline pulled out her chair and then paused, her gaze following the bald man who was making his way to the bar. She nudged Linda. "Do you know that guy? The one with the shaved head and green scarf?"

Linda leaned to the left and squinted. "Never saw him before in my life. Could be a new Evergreen employee. Why?"

"He came into the store the other day. Bought a frog."

"You don't still think Larry is sending spies out here, do you?"

Linda raised her brows in a way that made Caroline flush three different heat levels. She had to suffer through those looks if she wanted to keep up the pretense of the abusive husband. Neither Linda nor Cole would think she was so silly and paranoid if they knew her real reason for being in Timberline and jumping at every loud noise.

"He just seemed suspicious." Caroline flicked open the menu and sniffed. "I know it's ridiculous. I just can't help it."

Linda's face softened. "I know, dear. You have every right to be on edge. I don't know the man, but I can find out who he is. Even with Evergreen setting up shop, Timberline is still a small town and I have my sources."

That inconvenient guilt niggled in her belly. It had never occurred to Linda that Caroline might be lying about everything and that Cole could be, as well. The man with the shaved head could be lying to the bartender right now.

Chloe, their waitress, came up to the table, tapping her pencil against her notebook. "Hi, ladies. What can I get you tonight? Start you off with a glass of wine?"

"That sounds perfect." Linda nudged Caroline's arm. "Let's indulge, just one and I'm driving."

Caroline hadn't had any alcohol since she'd been born in that motel room, but surely she could stop at one and not fall into an alcohol-induced conversation with Linda.

"I'm in. I'll have the house white, whatever that is."

Chloe raised her pencil in the air. "It's a chardonnay from the Willamette Valley. Is that okay?"

"That's fine."

"And you'll have the same, Linda?"

"Yes, thank you, Chloe."

"Do you want me to bring a carafe?"

"Oh no, just a glass for each of us is fine."

As Chloe turned from the table, a twentysomething man with long black hair caught in a ponytail nudged her back. "I need to talk to you. Now."

She brushed him off. "I'm working here, Jason."

"Hello, Jason." Linda gave the young man a smile.

"Hi, Ms. Gunderson. Sorry to interrupt." He nudged Chloe in the back again.

"We can wait for our wine. Have you met my cousin Caroline Johnson?"

Jason held up one hand. "Nice to meet you, ma'am."

"Go see what Jason wants, Chloe."

As Jason and Chloe wandered away, heads together, Linda took a sip of water. "Those two are such a nice couple. Jason's Quileute, from the reservation. Hardworking young man."

Caroline covered a smile with one hand. Linda obviously enjoyed seeing love flourish.

When Chloe came back with their wine, her smooth brow was creased with worry.

Linda didn't seem to notice and Caroline didn't know Chloe well enough to inquire, so they ordered their food.

Caroline kept up the conversation with Linda while glancing toward the bar every once in a while. The bald guy hadn't spoken to anyone except the bartender, Denny, and didn't seem to be meeting anyone, since he'd already started eating his burger.

Linda had drained her wineglass, and when Chloe returned to deliver their food, she ordered a second glass.

"I'm eating a big meal." Linda waved her fork over her plate, which was overflowing with a thick pork chop and mashed potatoes and gravy. "I should be okay to drive."

"If you say so." Caroline took a sip of water and tossed her napkin on the table. "I'm going to use the restroom. I'll be right back."

She scooted back from the table and veered toward the perimeter of the room. She glanced over her shoulder before entering the short hallway to the bathrooms and the exit.

The man at the bar was still eating and hadn't noticed her. She washed her hands at the sink and took a deep breath before stepping into the hallway. She flattened herself against the wall and hunched forward a little until she could see the bar.

She didn't know what she hoped to discover about the man from here. She'd gotten lucky the night she'd overheard Cole on his cell phone. Luck like that wouldn't strike twice.

Nothing about the man screamed biker, drug trafficker or even cop.

So why had he made her senses spike? Because he'd been watching her from the end of the alley the night she'd suspected someone had broken into her place? The night of the pouring rain, when Cole had rescued her from the mud and had made everything okay?

She huffed softly through her nostrils. He was in law enforcement. That's what those guys did—set everything right again. Could he set her right again?

No. Once he discovered her identity, or at least what she knew of her identity, that hard, cold look would come into his eyes and they'd turn to green chips of ice.

A pretty blonde stopped next to the man with the shaved head and perched on the stool next to him, facing him. They chatted, heads together, and then she handed him some papers.

Maybe Linda could ID the blonde, Caroline thought. Before she could peel herself from the wall, Chloe and her boyfriend stumbled into the hallway, their voices harsh whispers as they argued about something.

Caroline cleared her throat. Two sets of eyes pinned her, so she gave a weak smile, eased out of the hall and scurried back to her table. She didn't want them to think she was eavesdropping. She had enough of her own problems.

Caroline widened her eyes when she saw a half carafe of wine in front of Linda, who was chatting with one of her card-playing friends.

"Here she is, my sweet cousin Caroline."

Caroline smiled at the other woman. "Irene, right?"

"You have a good memory."

Caroline coughed to mask the laugh bubbling from her throat. "Linda talks about her good friends all the time."

"Linda's lucky to have you here while her sister is gone. When is Louise coming back, Linda?"

"About two weeks."

"And while the cat's away the mouse will play." Irene tapped a fingernail against Linda's wineglass. Then leaned close to Caroline. "Louise doesn't like it when Linda has more than a glass of wine."

"Oh, stop it. Louise isn't my keeper." Linda waved her hand. "Stop causing trouble. I'll see you next week."

Irene winked at Caroline and left the restaurant.

"I can drive, Linda. Finish your wine and don't worry about it."

"If you think you can."

Caroline held up her water glass. "I just had the one glass, but you can do me a favor."

"Anything for my little cousin." Linda hiccupped and pressed her fingers against her lips.

The blonde had finished speaking to the man at the bar and had started making her way to the front door, stopping here and there along the way.

"Who's that attractive blonde in the skirt and heels?" Caroline tipped her head toward the woman.

"Where?" Linda twisted her head from side to side.

Nudging Linda's toe beneath the table, Caroline hissed, "Shh." She held up her hand and jabbed her palm with her index finger. "Right there, talking to that couple two tables over."

Linda hunched forward, slurring her speech. "That's Rebecca Geist. She's a Realtor, but she probably won't be here much longer. She's engaged to a very rich man. Besides…" Linda glanced both ways. "She was beaten up pretty badly a few months ago."

Caroline recoiled from the tinny odor of Linda's alcohol-infused breath. "Here in Timberline?"

"She was helping some woman, a TV reporter, who was doing a story on the Timberline Trio case. You know that show *Cold Case Chronicles*?"

Caroline nodded as if she did, although she'd never heard of it.

"Well, the host of that show only pretended to be doing a story on the Timberline Trio." Linda's voice was a harsh whisper, but the couple at the next table glanced over. "But she really thought she was one of kidnapped kids. She wasn't, but her snooping around got her into other trouble, and since Rebecca had been helping her, it got Rebecca in trouble, too."

A sharp pain lanced Caroline's left temple, and she massaged her head. "It seems as if that case never ended for this town."

"That's for sure, and I don't think it ever will, since the children were never found. That kind of thing haunts a town." With a shaky hand, Linda tipped more wine from the carafe into her glass. "We're cursed."

Caroline tapped the edge of Linda's plate with her fork. "Finish your pork chop. Do you want some of my fries from my fish and chips?"

"I think I have enough food here. I'll finish." She took another sip of wine.

Caroline toyed with the fries on her plate as she watched the Realtor leave the restaurant. The man with the shaved head was probably here to buy property or something. Maybe he was making the move to Timberline for a job at Evergreen. He'd told her he was here on business.

Caroline finished her dinner and five minutes later followed the progress of the man from the bar as he skirted the dining area on his way out of the restaurant. When he reached the hostess stand, he looked over his shoulder, meeting Caroline's gaze, a slight smile playing about his lips.

He turned and left before she could break eye contact. What did it mean? What interest could he possibly have in her? Unless—she gripped her fork so tightly her knuckles turned white—he was the one she was supposed to meet in Timberline.

That scrap of paper in her pocket with Timberline

written on it in her own handwriting had to have been there for a reason.

Maybe she should approach him. Maybe he had the answers she'd been seeking. He didn't seem menacing. She hadn't gotten that kind of vibe from him—except when he'd been watching her in the rain.

She dug a pen from her purse and scribbled down Rebecca Geist's name on a napkin. Perhaps she'd look into some Timberline real estate.

"Can we leave, Caroline? I'm so tired."

She looked across the table at Linda's drooping eyelids and mottled cheeks. "Of course, and don't even think about driving. You're downright tipsy."

"Am I?" Linda giggled.

Caroline couldn't get her out of there fast enough. Was Linda a blabbermouth drunk? Would she spill all her secrets?

A tall man came through the front door of the restaurant and the stakes just got higher.

"Look, there's Cole." Linda waved and called his name.

Caroline touched Chloe's arm as she passed their table. "We'd like the check, Chloe. Right away."

The waitress nodded absently. "I'll be right with you."

Cole made his way to their table and pulled out a chair. He lifted the carafe and swirled the sip of wine left in the bottom. "Looks like I missed the party."

"Party of one." Caroline rolled her eyes.

"I hope you don't plan to drive home, Linda."

"Caroline has offered, although I'm fine. I ate a lot."

Cole raised his brows at her half-eaten pork chop and pile of potatoes. "Yeah, I think you'd better give Caroline the keys."

Linda murmured, "My sweet cousin."

Caroline's stomach bunched into knots. "Excuse us if we don't hang around, Cole."

"That's okay. I'm just here for a pickup."

Since Chloe didn't seem to be returning anytime soon, Caroline pulled some cash from her wallet and dropped three twenties on the table as she scooted back her chair.

"You're not going to wait for the check?" Cole stood up when she did, and placed a hand on Linda's shoulder.

Snatching her jacket from the back of the empty chair, Caroline said, "That should cover it. Are you ready, Linda?"

"I think so." Linda had dropped her chin to her chest and closed her eyes.

Cole mouthed the words, *Do you need help?*

She shook her head. She didn't want to embarrass Linda and cause a scene.

She gripped Linda's upper arm. "Ready? One, two, three."

Linda rose to her feet unsteadily and bumped her shoulder against Caroline's.

"I'm just going to hang on to your arm through the restaurant. You'll feel better when you get some fresh air."

"Oh, do stop nagging me, Louise."

Caroline shrugged her shoulders at Cole. She had to get Linda out of here fast.

With just a few shuffled steps and a little bit of a stagger from Linda, Caroline managed to get her safely out of the restaurant without setting off too many wagging tongues.

If Chloe knew about Linda's fondness for chardonnay, chances were the rest of Timberline did, as well.

Caroline took Linda's keys from her purse and poured Linda into the passenger seat, snapping her seat belt in place. Then she did the same for herself.

As she pulled away from the curb, a motorcycle roared out of the alley and fishtailed on the wet asphalt before zooming off. Looked like Chloe's hot-headed boyfriend. Caroline tightened her hands on the steering wheel. She couldn't account for other drivers, but she always took care to drive safely, since she had no driver's license. At least she had only a mile to go and crazy Jason on the bike was long gone.

As her passenger snored softly beside her, Caroline pulled the car into Linda's side of the driveway. She nudged her shoulder. "Linda? We're home."

She parked and helped her from the car. The older woman leaned heavily against her and Caroline staggered up the two steps to the front door. She led Linda to her bedroom, where she kicked off both shoes after about five tries and then crawled under the covers fully clothed.

Caroline tucked the covers around her shoulders, then tiptoed to the bathroom, found a bottle of aspirin and shook a couple into her palm. After filling a glass with water from the tap in the kitchen, she put it and the two aspirin on Linda's nightstand.

If the woman woke up in the middle of the night, she might be able to stave off an even worse hangover by taking the aspirin.

Caroline grabbed her purse and hitched it over her shoulder. She studied Linda's key chain in the palm of her hand. Maybe she should keep the house key so she could lock the dead bolt from the outside.

She penned a note to Linda and then placed her set of keys on the piece of paper on a table by the front door.

Caroline pulled the door closed behind her, locked the dead bolt and pocketed Linda's house key. It was the least she could do for the woman who'd taken her in and lied for her.

A soft patter of rain caressed her cheek when she stepped off the porch. For a moment she lifted her face to the drops. The rain wasn't so bad, after all.

She began to cross the driveway to her own side of the duplex when a gruff voice behind her stopped her cold.

"Where's the money, bitch?"

Chapter Eight

Cole cracked open his car door as Caroline walked across the driveway to her own place. Looked like he'd come too late to help her with Linda. Caroline must be stronger than she looked or Linda had recovered some of her mobility.

He put his boot down on the gravel and heard voices. Had Linda followed Caroline outside? Then a man's voice carried into the street. "I said, where's the money, bitch?"

A surge of adrenaline rushed through Cole's body and he yelled, "Hey!"

As he rounded the front of his car, rushing toward the driveway, Caroline screamed. Cole slipped on some wet leaves and recovered his balance in time to see Caroline lurch forward onto her hands and knees in the middle of the driveway—alone.

He rushed to her side, his fingers curled around the butt of his gun in his pocket. "Are you injured? Did he hurt you?"

She shook her head. "No."

"Where is he? Where'd he go?"

With glassy eyes she pointed into the copse of trees, shrouded in darkness, on the other side of Linda's duplex.

"Get inside and lock the door. Call 911." He pulled her to her feet. Once the local cops got here, he'd have to reveal his true identity, but it would be worth it to nail the man who'd attacked Caroline.

She grabbed handfuls of his jacket. "H-he has a knife."

"I have a gun." He patted his pocket and then grabbed her hands and kissed them. "Go."

He watched her until she disappeared inside, then took off at a jog toward the blackest spot in his vision. He might have a gun but he didn't have a flashlight.

He pulled out his cell phone and swiped on the flashlight, holding the phone in front of him to light a small, pathetic path into the dense woods.

When he got to the edge of the tree line, he stopped, head to one side, and listened for any movement. Either the guy was hiding, concealed and silent, or he was long gone. Cole thrashed through the bushes and branches, stopping periodically to listen, but only a few birds twittered an answer.

He'd never find anyone out here and he risked getting knifed before he would ever be able to see the threat coming at him.

With his phone in one hand and his gun in the other, he made his way out of the forest and back to Caroline's front door. No sirens yet.

Could the man threatening her be connected to her husband? Maybe she had good reason to be paranoid, but why would he be asking her for money, unless she'd taken money from her husband when she escaped from him? So many things didn't add up about her—the woman of mystery.

He pocketed his gun and knocked on her door. "Caroline? It's me, Cole."

A chain scraped across its metal track and a dead bolt clicked before she inched the door open. Her face had yet to regain its color.

"Are you okay? Can I come in?"

The door widened and she stepped back. "I'm okay. Shaken, but okay. Did you find anything out there?"

"Too damned dark and I don't have a flashlight other than the one on my phone." He crossed the threshold. "What happened? I heard him ask for money. Was he trying to rob you?"

"I guess so." She shut the door and put both locks into place again. "I had just come out of Linda's house after putting her to bed and locking her door."

"He accosted you in the driveway? Because I saw you through the passenger window first, and I didn't see anyone else on the driveway."

"He came up behind me. Maybe he'd been hiding in the woods."

"Did you see him?"

"He told me not to turn around—and I didn't. He said he had a knife and then put it to my throat." She placed one hand around the column of her throat as if to protect it.

"What else did he say? When I got out of my car, I heard voices and then he shouted."

"The shout? That's pretty much what he said to me. He said 'Give me the money, bitch.' I started to turn, instinct I guess, and that's when he said he had a knife and he didn't want me to move. He put the blade to my flesh and then shouted again, and that's what you heard." She twisted her fingers in front of her. "When you yelled, he pushed me and I turned around, but only saw him plunging into the trees."

"How did he expect you to give him any money when he didn't want you to move?"

"I don't know." She hunched her shoulders. "Maybe he was going to grab my purse or something."

Cole rubbed both her arms from her shoulders to her elbows and back up again. "Your body is trembling. Sit down. Do you want some water? Tea?"

She moved like a zombie to the sofa against the wall and sank down on the end, clasping her hands between her knees. "Water maybe, thanks."

He strode into the kitchen and opened a few mostly empty cupboards before finding one with a single row of drinking glasses lined up. He lifted one from the shelf and filled it with water from the tap.

When he returned to the living room, he handed her the glass and then paced away from her. "Do you think this had anything to do with Larry?"

"Wh-why would it?"

He studied her face. Every other thing that had happened to her she'd put at the feet of Larry. Why back off from that stance now?

"You can tell me the truth, Caroline. Did you take some money from him? Is that why you've been so worried that he'd come after you?" Cole spread his hands. "I wouldn't blame you. The guy sounds like he had it coming."

Her doe eyes darted from the door to his face and back again, like she was an animal caught in a snare.

He took two steps toward the couch and sat on the cushion next to her. His weight on the soft sofa had her tilting toward him, her shoulder bouncing against his.

"It's okay." He put his arm around her, taking care not to draw her nearer—even though he wanted to. "You can tell me anything. I won't judge you. I told you, my mom got out of an abusive relationship, and if she'd stolen money from the SOB, my stepfather, our lives would've gone much more smoothly. Hell, it was probably just as much your money as his, so you didn't really steal it."

Her body stiffened. "I—I did take money out of our accounts, but it was mine, too. I guess he tracked me here to Timberline. He must've been paying closer attention to my chatter about relatives than I thought he was. He remembered the Gundersons from Timberline and sent someone out here to find me. It probably wasn't hard. Everyone here knows I'm Linda's second cousin. Everyone knows I'm Caroline Johnson. Larry's cohort probably got Linda's address, and waited for us to come home. He got me alone and jumped on the opportunity. I'm going to have to leave Timberline."

Cole dropped his arm from her shoulders and rubbed his jaw. That rapid-fire response was the most he'd gotten out of Caroline since the day he'd met her.

"That was my first thought—that this had something

to do with your husband. But why would this guy, this friend of Larry's, approach you this way? Why wouldn't he just knock on your door and tell you that Larry expected his money back or he'd see you in court? Technically, when you initiate divorce proceedings, neither party is supposed to touch any of the common funds. Believe me, I speak from experience. Of course, each state is different, but what are the rules in…? Where are you from, exactly?"

"Now you think this is some random attack? Just some thug holding me up for cash?"

Cole pressed his thumbs against either side of his head. "I don't know. It just doesn't make sense that Larry would send someone else out here to get his money. If he knew where you were, wouldn't Larry come to Timberline himself to confront you?"

"That's not Larry. He'd send someone else to do his dirty work."

"Is that why you didn't call the police?" With his shoulder still pressed against hers, he felt her body jerk. "You didn't call, right? They would've been here by now. Most people I know rush to call 911 when something like this happens."

Closing her eyes, she leaned against the back of the sofa. A pulse beat wildly in her throat. "Please don't call them. I'll call Larry myself and tell him I'll return the money. I don't want the police involved. I don't want to cause any trouble in Timberline."

Cole scanned her face, the parted lips, lashes fluttering against the smooth skin of her cheeks. A tear slid from the corner of one of her eyes, traveled to her hairline and meandered toward her ear.

Was that tear even real? Did anything she'd told him since the day he'd met her at the library have one kernel of truth in it?

She sniffled and rubbed her eyes as she sat forward. "Please. I'd rather handle this my own way."

"Which is what? Leave Timberline for parts unknown?" His voice sounded harsh to his own ears and Caroline flinched at the tone.

He didn't know if he was angry at her for lying or angry at himself for getting taken in by a pretty face and a sad story—again. Or even worse, was he angry because she was leaving?

He was *not* telling his sister about this one. She'd start to have doubts about whether he could date without supervision—not that Caroline had ever been dating material, though he'd wanted her to be. He could be a man and admit that, even admit he'd been a fool.

"I think that's best, don't you?" She grabbed his arm and turned those big, baby blue eyes on him.

He shook her off. "Do what you want, Caroline. I think you've been lying to me from the get-go."

Her face drained of all color and she jerked back from him.

"I don't know what your game is with your husband and his so-called friend. I don't know if he's abusive or if you told that story to your cousin so she'd take you in. Who knows?" Cole jumped up from the sofa to get away from the scent of her flowery perfume. "Maybe it's all a scam you two are running to get money out of Linda and Louise."

Caroline emitted a strangled cry and covered her mouth with both hands.

He turned away and walked toward the window. "All I do know is not calling the sheriff's department after someone pulls a knife on you is a huge red flag. You didn't realize that a DEA agent, of all people, wouldn't be suspicious about that?"

She gulped down the water he'd brought her and wiped her mouth with the back of her hand. "Actually, I thought you'd be relieved to keep the cops out of it, since you'd have to come clean about who you are and what you're doing in Timberline."

"Is that a threat? 'Cuz bring it on." He spread his arms out to his sides. "You can go ahead and tell everyone in town that I'm DEA. You know the funniest thing about it? I'd realized my cover would be blown, but I figured it would be worth it to keep you safe. Pretty funny, huh?"

She dropped her gaze from his and another tear slid from the same eye. She must've perfected the art of crying from one eye only. She'd have to work on the tear ducts for that other eye.

"That's not funny at all. I'm grateful and humbled you'd feel that way."

His heart lurched—just a little—and then he widened his stance and crossed his arms. "Yeah, another sucker."

Rolling the glass between her hands, she rose from the sofa and sauntered to the kitchen to place it on the counter. He tried like hell to keep his eyes off her rounded hips as they swung from side to side, and her long, tangled, toffee-brown hair tumbling down her back.

She turned suddenly and his gaze jumped to her face. "I'm not going to do it."

"Do what? Scam Linda? Leave town? Give your husband his money back?"

"Blow your cover."

"Whatever. Do what you have to do. I'm not hanging around much longer, anyway. This was a wild-goose chase for me."

Except for meeting Caroline, this investigation had been a bust. The single female in the cabin hadn't fit the description of the woman at the Stardust at all. Only Caroline had come close in appearance and general arrival time to Timberline, and her cousin Linda had vouched for her already.

Caroline's visit to the therapist had also thrown him for a loop. There would be no reason for Johnny's murderer or girlfriend or accomplice to head to Timberline and see a therapist.

"I'm not a bad person, Cole. I mean, I don't *feel* like I'm a bad person." She folded her hands in front of her. "I'm not trying to…scam Linda."

"Whatever is going on between family members is their business. I'm out. I don't need to be involved anymore. I'm not going to rat you out to the police, or Linda or Larry or Larry's many friends, real or imagined."

"I appreciate that…and everything you've done for me." Caroline tipped her chin toward the window. "You saved me out there. You comforted me the other night when I thought someone had broken in. You're a good guy, Cole Pierson."

"That's me." He thumped his chest twice with his fist. "The good guy."

Caroline's cell phone rang.

"Better get that. It's probably your accomplice." He stalked toward the front door and whipped off the chain.

Caroline's voice, high-pitched and breathy, stopped him. "Linda? What's wrong? Oh, my God. Hang on. I'll be right over."

He'd turned at the door and watched Caroline as she swiped a key from the countertop and grabbed her jacket.

"What's the matter with Linda?"

"I'm not sure. She's sick, vomiting, and she collapsed on the floor when she tried to get out of bed. I'm going over to help her. C-can you call 911?"

"I will, but I'm coming over with you. I have some first-aid training as part of my job."

She nodded and flew out the front door.

He followed, phone in hand, calling 911.

And just like that, he'd been swept back into the helter-skelter world of Caroline Johnson—or whatever the hell her name was.

Chapter Nine

Caroline paced back and forth across the hospital's emergency waiting room. "I didn't think she was that drunk. Maybe it's been a while and it hit her wrong."

"She's getting up there in age, and it looked like she drank a lot on an empty stomach. Bad combination." Cole patted the plastic chair next to him. "Have a seat."

Caroline glanced over her shoulder at his worried face. Just when she thought he was going to walk out of her life for good, he'd been a steady rock when they'd found Linda semiconscious on the floor of her bedroom, choking on her vomit. He'd taken control of the situation. He'd known just what to do and had probably saved Linda's life.

While Caroline had been a babbling idiot, he'd explained everything to the EMTs as they worked on Linda and loaded her into the ambulance.

Then, instead of abandoning her, he'd driven Caroline to the emergency room, following the ambulance and getting her settled in the waiting room. He did all that and he hated her. Imagine what a man like that would do for someone he loved.

She plopped onto the chair next to him, stretching her legs in front of her. The only silver lining from that entire episode in the driveway was that Cole clearly still believed she was Linda's cousin and had nothing to do with Johnny Diamond. That was the *only* good that came out of it.

Of course she couldn't call the Timberline Sheriff's Department. They'd have wanted her name, driver's license, information about her mythical husband, Larry. It was one thing telling a few lies here and there around town, but she couldn't put herself in the hands of the police—not now. She needed a few more sessions with Dr. Shipman.

Cole put a steadying hand on her bouncing knee. "Linda's going to be okay. She overindulged, got… snockered, got sick and didn't have enough fluids in her body. They'll hook her up to an IV and she'll be fine."

"I'm so glad she was able to get to her phone and call me. She could've died."

"She knew she could count on you."

"Really?" Caroline slid a glance at him from the corner of her eye. "I thought I was trying to scam her."

His jaw formed a hard line, as if she'd just reminded him he couldn't trust her.

She bit her lip. She should just shut up about all that instead of trying to prove something to Cole. In a sense, he was right. She'd been lying to Linda since the day she met her behind the shop. She'd taken advantage of her good and sympathetic nature, all the while hiding her true intentions.

Cole lifted one shoulder. "Okay, maybe I was harsh

earlier. You're here now, and I'm not going to say another word about it."

She rubbed her eyes. "You said a few things back there. You're divorced?"

"Another statistic."

"But you don't have children. You mentioned that in the store the other day."

"One of my regrets, but since the marriage ended I suppose it's a good thing we didn't bring kids into the mix."

"How'd it end?" He'd left his hand on her knee and she traced a finger across his knuckles. "I'm sorry. You don't owe me any explanations."

He flexed his fingers. "I don't mind. In some ways it's easier opening up to the woman of mystery. You know nothing about her, so you won't read any judgment in her eyes or tone."

Caroline snatched her hand away and stuffed it in her jacket pocket. "Like I said, you don't have to tell me anything."

"She cheated on me."

"That's awful. I'm sorry." Was his wife crazy? Hot, sexy, steady. What more could you ask for in a man?

"With a drug dealer."

This time Caroline couldn't contain her surprise. Her mouth dropped open. "You're kidding."

"I wish I was."

"Did she pick him on purpose? I mean, what are the odds that she'd fall into the arms of one of her husband's natural enemies?"

"Natural enemy. I like that." Cole stretched and

yawned, obviously no longer bothered by the incident…
or hiding it well. "It's complicated."

"Is it someone she knew before you?"

"Exactly. Wendy ran with a wild crowd. I met her
at a club while I was working undercover. I just didn't
realize she was in so deep with the bunch we were investigating. Bust went down and I ran into her about
six months later, getting her life together, she said."

"So, she fell hard for the straight-arrow DEA agent.
She liked the domesticated lifestyle for a while and then
started to get the itch," Caroline murmured.

Cole leveled a finger at her. "You're good. One session with that therapist and you've got it all figured out."

"Is that what happened?"

"Yeah. I discovered what was going on pretty fast.
She'd been with the dude once, and I knew it right
away." Cole hit his forehead with the heel of his hand.
"God, she could've ruined my career."

"It's a good thing you got out of that marriage when
you did."

"Uh-huh." He tipped back his head and stared at
the ceiling.

As Cole got lost in thoughts of the past, Caroline
twirled a strand of hair around her finger. No wonder
he'd gone ballistic on her when she refused to call the
police. She thought she'd had him fooled, but he never
really trusted her.

He couldn't nab her for Johnny's accomplice, but
he'd known something wasn't right about her. He didn't
want to get tricked by another wild woman, and she
didn't blame him.

God, she must've come across exactly like his ex—troubled, needy, looking for a white knight. Cole Pierson could totally deliver in the white knight category, but he'd want to know his damsel really needed rescuing and wasn't running a con.

Caroline wasn't, but she'd have to tell him the truth to explain everything—and she wasn't ready to do that. So he'd go his way and she'd go hers, whatever that way turned out to be.

She'd have to leave Timberline unless she wanted another experience like tonight's. She didn't think for one minute the encounter in her driveway was a random incident.

Give me the money, bitch.

That could mean only one thing. Johnny Diamond's business partners somehow knew she'd lifted some cash from the duffel bag. But how? The police had those bags—the cash and the drugs. How would Johnny's associates know about the missing money? That wasn't the type of information the authorities would release. Had the accounts of Johnny's murder mentioned drugs or money at all? Must've mentioned drugs, because everyone knew he was a drug dealer.

She sucked in her bottom lip and chewed it. Maybe Johnny's cohorts believed she'd taken all the money. That could be bad—really bad.

And how did these guys even know who she was or what she looked like? *Rocky.* Rocky, the kidnapper of little children, somehow knew who she was.

Her stomach rolled with nausea. She had to get out of here.

The emergency room doors swung open and Chloe from Sutter's and her boyfriend, Jason, came into the waiting room. Jason was holding up a bloodied and broken hand.

Caroline clutched the arms of the chair. Had he done that on Chloe's face? Caroline shifted her gaze to Chloe, who gave her a half smile and a shrug. "Boys being boys."

Whatever that meant, but at least Chloe didn't show any signs of abuse. Maybe Jason had hit the wall in anger—better than hitting Chloe.

The doors to the examination rooms swung open and the doc on duty strode across the waiting room, never looking up from his clipboard. "Ms. Johnson?"

She shot out of the plastic chair and Cole jumped up beside her. "I'm Caroline Johnson."

"You're—" he flipped a page over on his clipboard "—the cousin. Ms. Gunderson is going to be fine. She was dehydrated, weak and extremely intoxicated. We're getting some fluids into her right now and she's resting. Because of her age, we're keeping her overnight."

Caroline sighed and caught Cole's arm. "She's going to be okay?"

"She'll be fine, but I've warned her to lay off the booze in the future. Her body can't handle it. She wants to see you, but don't tire her out. She'll be released tomorrow."

"Thank you, Dr…?"

He nodded once, dropped the clipboard at the front desk and shouted out a few orders before disappearing behind the swinging doors.

The nurse at reception rolled her eyes. "That's Dr. Nesbitt—busy man. Stella will take you back to see Linda."

"Thanks." Caroline tugged on the hem of Cole's jacket. "Do you want to go back with me?"

"I'm sure Linda doesn't want me there when she's not feeling well. Give her my best, and I'll be waiting here for you."

"Thanks, Cole. I won't be long. The charming Dr. Nesbitt said she needed her rest."

One corner of his mouth lifted. "I never got to eat my dinner tonight. I'm going to get a candy bar from the vending machine. Take your time."

Caroline pushed open one of the doors and a nurse in a pink lab coat met her with a big smile. "I'm Stella. Follow me."

Caroline followed Stella's comforting pink form down a hallway past a few curtained off areas until she stopped at an open door. She tapped. "Linda, Caroline's here to see you."

Linda was so white, she practically blended in with the sheets, and Caroline rushed to her bedside. "Are you feeling better? I was scared to death, but Dr. Nesbitt said you're going to be okay."

Linda looked at her with a pair of watery eyes and a deep furrow between her eyebrows. "I felt like I was going to die."

"I'm so sorry." Caroline took her clammy hand in hers. "I should've never left you in that condition."

"How could you know I'd react that way?" She covered her eyes with her free hand, which was trembling.

"It was so foolish. I'm glad Louise wasn't here to witness it."

"We all do foolish things." Caroline smoothed the crisp sheet over Linda's thigh. "Are you comfortable here? They're keeping you overnight. Do you want me to bring you anything?"

"N-no. I'll try to get some sleep." Linda glanced over Caroline's shoulder at the open door and dropped her voice to a whisper. "Did that young doctor say anything about what caused my illness?"

Caroline began to organize the items on the small tray next to the bed. "You drank too much wine, Linda, became ill and then got dehydrated."

"Oh." Linda sank back against her pillow. "Would you believe me if I told you that's never happened to me before, Caroline?"

"Of course. Sometimes things hit us funny." She drew her eyebrows together. "What are you driving at?"

"I felt ill, really, really ill. It hit me before I even left the restaurant." Linda put her hand over her mouth and murmured, "I don't even remember leaving the restaurant. I didn't make a scene, did I?"

"Not at all." She patted the older woman's hand. "I guided you out of there and nobody noticed a thing."

"I'm not trying to make excuses, but I wonder if I had a touch of food poisoning."

"Really? Maybe that's why you didn't finish your meal. But doesn't it usually take a few hours before the symptoms of food poisoning appear? It doesn't happen immediately, does it?"

"I don't know, but something didn't feel right."

"I can check with Sutter's tomorrow to find out if there were any other complaints."

"Would you?" Linda clutched her hand in a weak grip. "I'm so glad I had you to call on, Caroline. You more than paid me back for any assistance I've given you since you came to Timberline. You'll stay for a while, won't you? You've truly become like a daughter to me."

Tears stung Caroline's nose. How could she tell her she was ready to hightail it out of town? "I'll stay until Louise comes back, at least."

"Is that all?" The corners of Linda's mouth drooped. "You're welcome to start over here. We'd love to have you."

"You know what?" Caroline pulled the sheets up to Linda's chin. "You're tired. Get some rest, and I'll be back to pick you up tomorrow when they spring you from this joint."

Linda gave her a weak smile. "And Cole?"

Caroline snapped her fingers. "I almost forgot. Here I am, basking in your gratitude, and you owe your life to Cole. He was with me when you called, and he came over to help out. He cleared your air passages while we were waiting for the EMTs."

A hot red blush flooded Linda's pale cheeks. "Oh, for Cole to see me like that. I'm mortified."

Caroline laughed. "You have such a crush on that man. He was so relieved he could be there to help, and he sends his best wishes."

A small smile settled on Linda's lips and her eyes fluttered closed.

Caroline squeezed her hands and whispered, "Sweet dreams."

She tiptoed from the room and thanked Stella in the hallway. Blowing out a breath, she pushed through the double doors to the waiting room. "You're right. She would've been *mortified*, her words, if you'd gone back there and seen her bedridden."

"She's doing okay?"

"She's fine, embarrassed and…"

"And what?" Cole steered her toward his rental car and hit the key fob.

Caroline leaned against the passenger door, crossing her arms. "She said her reaction to the wine was uncharacteristic for her."

"I'd hope so."

"Said she'd never felt that way before and thought it might even have been food poisoning."

"Really?" Cole tossed his keys in the air and caught them in his palm. "Did Dr. Speedy in there run any kind of tests on her?"

"I—I don't know. What kind of tests?" Caroline dug her fingers into her biceps.

"Toxicology."

"Toxicology?" A chill had crept across her flesh, and she hunched her shoulders. Didn't toxicology tests reveal poisons in the system? She didn't want to have that discussion with Cole.

"I don't think so." She yanked open the car door and practically dived inside. "It's cold out here."

By the time Cole got around to the driver's side and

cranked on the engine and the heat, he seemed to have forgotten about toxicology tests.

"Are you still heading out of town?"

"I want to, but I can't leave Linda to fend for herself right now. Maybe once she recovers, I'll think about it."

"You should. If your assailant in the driveway was here on your husband's behalf and wasn't a random robber, then your hiding place has been compromised." Cole held one hand out to the side. "And that's all I'm going to say on that subject."

For a brief time she'd forgotten about the man demanding money. Her previous questions lingered. How did they know about the missing money? How did they know where to find her? How did they know who she was?

Could the man have been someone who followed her and Linda from Sutter's, thinking they were both drunk and easy targets?

What about the man with the shaved head? Caroline braced her forehead against the cold glass of the window and went cross-eyed watching the dribbles of water on the pane.

Cross-eyed—that's how she felt right now. She didn't know what direction was up.

"You've had quite a day. Are you going to be okay?"

"Do you care?" She sealed her lips. Why did she feel compelled to goad him? It bugged her that he thought poorly of her, but she couldn't control that as long as she continued to lie to him about her situation. She had to pay that price, but it was getting to be an awfully high price to pay.

He let her question hang in the air between them until he pulled into the driveway of the duplex next to Linda's car.

As she reached for the door handle, he said, "I want you to be okay, Caroline, despite everything...even though I might be a damned fool." He leaned across the console, slipped his hand behind her head and kissed her hard on the mouth.

When he released her, breathless, lips throbbing, he said, "Just call me a damned fool."

She scrambled from his car and hurried to her front door, one hand pressed against her hot cheek.

If he was a damned fool for kissing her, what did that make her for liking it?

THE FOLLOWING MORNING, Caroline called the hospital to find out how Linda was doing and what time she'd be released. They wanted to hold her for the morning, so Caroline decided to pay a visit to Rebecca Geist, the Realtor the bald guy had talked to at the bar.

She drove Linda's car to Rebecca's office with the memory of Cole's kiss on her lips. They seemed drawn to each other even though they both sensed the danger that such an attraction presented. Caroline understood the danger from him and he only sensed it from her, but it didn't seem to matter. If she could spar with and play cat and mouse with Cole all day, she'd be one happy cat...or mouse. She never knew who was who and which was which. They were both a little bit cat and a little bit mouse.

And she was a little bit crazy to even go near the DEA agent investigating the murder of Johnny Diamond.

She parked in front of the Realtor's office and wandered inside as if she were actually interested in buying a place in Timberline.

Rebecca was chattering away on the phone a mile a minute and waved as Caroline walked through the door.

As the conversation continued, Caroline thumbed through some listings and got herself a cup of water from the dispenser.

Rebecca finally ended the call and stood up, straightening her slim skirt. "Sorry about that. I'm Rebecca Geist."

Caroline crossed the room and shook the woman's hand, fighting off a grimace at her firm grip. "Caroline Johnson."

Rebecca leveled a long, coral-tipped fingernail at her. "Linda Gunderson's niece, right?"

"Cousin, second cousin."

"That's right. Are you looking to stay here in Timberline? Get your own place? That's a sweet little piece of property the Gunderson sisters own, that duplex at the end of Main Street. It's a great location. I know neither of those ladies has children. Is that going to be yours one day?"

Caroline swallowed. So Cole wasn't the only one who thought she'd come to town to wiggle her way into an inheritance. Did everyone else believe that? She rolled her shoulders. Would she rather they believe she'd come here straight from a motel room containing the dead body of a drug dealer?

She shrugged. "Not that I know of. That's why I'm here. I'd like to get an idea of available properties and the pricing."

"There aren't a whole lot of residential properties on the market right now." Rebecca tapped her long finger-nails against the blotter. "There's that one cabin with the dead body."

The pen Caroline had been toying with flipped out of her fingers. "A dead body?"

"Turns out one of the town hotshots murdered his mistress years ago and stuffed her body in the chimney of a cabin he owned."

"I wouldn't be interested in that." Caroline crouched down to pick up the pen and press her hand against her galloping heart for a second or two.

"I think that's the only cabin available right now. The Kennedy cabin is vacant and will be going on the market soon, but the owner left town for a while."

Rebecca pulled a binder from the bookshelf next to her desk and shuffled through a few plastic-coated pages. "There are some big houses for sale, close to Evergreen Software, but those are more for families and Evergreen employees. Would you be interested in looking at one of those? Three thousand square feet minimum with at least four bedrooms and two bathrooms."

"That's huge. No, I was more interested in one of the cabins." Caroline ran her fingertip along one of the flyers for the big Evergreen Development homes.

Maybe the guy with the shaved head was looking at one of these. He did mention a daughter. Or was that a lie?

She closed the binder. "Do you have many people looking at those right now?"

"Not many. Evergreen's still doing well, but they're currently in a hiring freeze."

This trip had been a bust. She was no closer to learning the identity of the bald man than when she'd walked through the door. "Well, thanks for your time."

"My pleasure." Rebecca held out her business card between two fingers. "Let me know if you have any more questions."

Caroline took the card and slipped it into her purse. She turned toward the door and took a few steps before stopping and taking a deep breath. "I think I saw you at Sutter's last night."

"That was me, picking up some food. My fiancé lives in New York, so I do that a lot. Work late, eat at my desk."

"You were talking to a man at the bar." Caroline turned slightly to the side. "Shaved head, thirtyish. He looked familiar."

"Oh?" Rebecca's eyebrows snapped together. "You didn't grow up here, did you? Your cousins aren't true locals."

Did Rebecca look annoyed? "No. This is actually my first visit to Timberline."

"He's just an out-of-town client. Unless you're from Connecticut, I doubt you know him."

"I guess not." Caroline waved. "Thanks again."

When she got to Linda's car, she sat in the driver's

seat, hands on the wheel, staring straight ahead. There had been something odd about Rebecca's response. Caroline could understand wanting to protect the confidentiality of a client, but buying real estate wasn't the same as getting cosmetic surgery.

And why had Rebecca asked her about being a local? Had she been implying her client was a local? Couldn't be a local from Connecticut.

Leaning forward, Caroline bumped her forehead against the steering wheel. This man had just become a distraction from all her other problems.

A man had pulled a knife on her last night, demanding money, and she didn't know if the encounter was related to Diamond or not. Linda had fallen ill and needed her, even though she wanted to leave. And Cole had kissed her—after admitting he didn't trust her any more than he'd trusted his cheating wife.

She'd better watch her back while she stayed in Timberline caring for Linda, and she'd better watch her heart around Cole Pierson.

Her phone buzzed and she grabbed it from the console, checking the display. "Hello, Dr. Shipman."

"Hi, Caroline. Have any more memories come to you since our previous session?"

"I did sort of spontaneously say I liked the dry heat of the desert. I'm not sure if that was just the power of suggestion from the hypnosis or a true memory from my past."

"Interesting. Did it feel real?"

"It did, yes."

"The reason I'm calling is because I need to go out

of town the day after tomorrow, and I didn't want to cancel our appointment without giving you a chance to reschedule earlier. Tomorrow is usually a day off for me, but I'm trying to schedule some make-up appointments. Can you make it tomorrow in the morning or later in the afternoon around five o'clock?"

Linda's friends had already told her they were swooping in tomorrow to bring Linda some dinner and play some cards. "Five o'clock would work."

"Great. I'll see you then."

Caroline dropped the phone in the cup holder and started the engine. She couldn't wait to dig into her past once again with Dr. Shipman, but first she needed to take care of some business in the present, and that meant collecting Linda from the hospital and putting her crazy investigation of the man with the shaved head on hold.

By the time she arrived at the hospital, she'd convinced herself that the attack last night was a random act, the guy with the shaved head was really just here on business and that she'd have her life back after just one more session with Dr. Shipman.

And that she'd allow Cole to kiss her once more before he left town.

Linda didn't seem to share her optimistic outlook this morning, as she was sitting on the edge of the bed with her head down and her hands clasped between her knees.

"Ready to blow this joint? Had enough of Jell-O and daytime TV?"

"Yes, get me out of here."

Caroline crouched in front of Linda. "Are you okay? You seem...down."

"I'm fine, Caroline. Let's go."

"Do I need to talk to Dr. Nesbitt?"

"He's not even here. I've signed all their forms and turned over all my insurance information." She held out a handful of papers to Caroline. "I'm supposed to stay hydrated and rest."

"Then let's get you hydrated and resting."

The nurses insisted Linda leave in a wheelchair, so Caroline pushed her into the waiting room. When they got through the doors, Stella, the nurse from last night, called after them. "Caroline? I have a prescription for Linda at the desk."

"Okay." She squeezed Linda's shoulder. "I'll be right back."

When she got to the front desk, Stella hunched forward, sliding the prescription across the counter. "Just a heads-up. Linda's feeling a little out of sorts. Maybe it's just embarrassment."

"Thanks." Caroline shoved the prescription in her back pocket and returned to Linda. "I parked close. Do you want to walk or wheelchair it all the way?"

"I can walk."

She pushed the wheelchair outside and tried to help Linda to her feet, although the older woman brushed off her helping hand.

Stella wasn't kidding. Caroline had never seen Linda in a bad mood or even mildly upset before.

She opened the car door for her, settled her and then

hopped into the driver's seat. When she'd shut her own door, she asked, "Do you want to tell me what's wrong?"

"You'll just think I'm crazy, like all the rest of them in there."

"I swear I won't."

"I think I was poisoned last night."

Chapter Ten

A rash of goose bumps raced across Caroline's arms. "What?"

"Last night. I don't think I had that much wine. I was ill, sick. I was poisoned."

"You mean like food poisoning? Did you ask Dr. Nesbitt how long that would take to hit you?"

"Dr. Nesbitt, that young fool."

"What does that even mean, Linda? Are you talking about food poisoning?"

"I'm talking about poisoning poisoning. I think someone poisoned my food or wine last night."

Caroline hung on to the steering wheel as her mind spun out of control. Poison. More poison? Was someone out there trying to frame her? What were the odds that two people she'd been hanging out with had both ingested poison?

Could she be some kind of whacked-out person who poisoned other people and then blacked out? Caroline pinched the bridge of her nose, squeezing her eyes shut. She hadn't blacked out last night.

Could someone have poisoned the wine, thinking

she'd be the one drinking it? Had the poison been meant for her and not Linda?

Wait. What poison? This was all speculation on Linda's part.

"Did the hospital run any tests for that? Any toxicology tests?" Cole had suggested that last night. If he found out about Linda's suspicions, would he tie Caroline to Johnny Diamond again?

"The hospital and that quack doctor didn't believe me. I saw them snickering behind their hands. The old broad couldn't handle her booze and is making excuses."

"I'm sure they weren't thinking that."

"And I'm sure they were." Linda adjusted her seat belt and closed her eyes. "Just take me home."

Wrinkling her nose and checking the rearview mirror, Caroline started the car and pulled out of the hospital parking lot. "Linda?"

"Yes?"

"Why would someone try to poison you?"

"Why would someone break into your house?"

The steering wheel slipped out of her hands. "I—I don't think anyone did. I was overreacting that night. Do you think the poison was meant for me? Is that what you're trying to say?"

"Is he after you, Caroline? Is your husband stalking you?"

She hunched over the steering wheel and squinted at the road. How should she respond to that? As far as she knew, she had no husband. But someone could very well be stalking her, chasing after her for the money she stole from Johnny.

Maybe the cops had put out the word that empty bags were found with Johnny's body and they suspected that the bags had contained drugs and money. Maybe the cops, the DEA, wanted Johnny's associates to come after her and do their work for them. Maybe Cole was here to sweep up the refuse.

Caroline dragged in a shuddering breath and blew it out. "I don't think so, Linda, but you're right. My presence here is putting you in danger. Once I get you settled, I'll be on my way."

Linda sniffled and dabbed her nose with a tissue. "I didn't mean it like that, dear. I'm worried about you."

"And I'm worried about you. Do you want to take your suspicions to the sheriff's department? I can't believe the hospital just ignored you."

"Oh, you know doctors. They always think they know best, and I'm not setting myself up for the same type of ridicule from those fresh-faced sheriffs, either."

"Should I talk to the bartenders last night, or Chloe, to see if they noticed anyone suspicious hanging around?" Rebecca's mysterious client had been at the bar last night. Did he have an opportunity to put something in the wine?

Caroline's head throbbed with all the possibilities and scenarios—none of them good. She wished her appointment with Dr. Shipman was this afternoon. She couldn't stand to be in the dark one more night.

"I've gone and worried you, haven't I? I should've

kept my mouth shut. I didn't mean to say anything to you at all, but those doctors made me so mad."

"I'm sorry if you've been swept up in any of my craziness. You've been nothing but kind to me, but I really think I've worn out my welcome." Caroline held up her hand as Linda started to interrupt. "I have an appointment with Dr. Shipman tomorrow. I'm going to ask her for a referral to a therapist in a big city somewhere, and I'm going to take myself and my problems out of your hair."

"Caroline, I never meant to drive you off with my silliness."

"Poisoning isn't silliness."

"I'm not even sure that's what happened. I'm probably just an old fool who drank too much wine."

"I've been thinking about leaving, anyway. I can't stay here. It was always a temporary solution."

"And Cole?"

Heat surged to her cheeks. "What about Cole? I told you I wasn't ready for a romantic relationship."

"I know. It's such a shame you two couldn't have met at another time, in another place. He's a catch."

Another time and place? She had no other time and no other place. She had no past, no family, no life. The truth of it all punched her in the gut, and she could dissolve into a flood of tears right now if she weren't driving Linda home.

She'd never allowed herself a good cry. Maybe she just wasn't the crying type, but then what type was she? She didn't have a clue.

What had happened to all the hope and optimism

she'd felt on her way to the hospital? If someone had really tried to poison her and mistakenly poisoned Linda instead, she was in big trouble. Maybe the man in the driveway was expecting an easier time of it with a drugged-out victim. She had to get away.

When they got to the duplex, Caroline helped Linda wash up and change clothes. Then she led her to her favorite chair. "Tea, water, glass of wine?"

Linda chuckled. "If you're here when Louise gets back, and I hope you are, please don't tell her about this. She can be insufferably self-righteous."

"Not a word from me." Caroline ran her fingertip over the seam of her lips. "How about that tea?"

"I'd love some if you'll join me. What did you do this morning before you picked me up?"

Caroline called over her shoulder as she filled the tea kettle with water. "I cleaned up my place and went to the library."

The lie came easily to her lips, but she didn't want to worry Linda about her obsession with the man from Connecticut.

"You didn't see Cole?"

"Not this morning." She ran her tongue along her bottom lip. Not that she hadn't been thinking about him and that kiss all day.

"Well, he's here now."

She dropped the kettle onto the burner. "Here?"

"He just drove up."

He tapped on Linda's door seconds later, and Caroline wiped her hands on a dish towel and answered the door.

"Linda home safely?"

"She is." She swung open the door. "See for yourself."

"Feeling better, beautiful?" Cole swept a bouquet of flowers from behind his back, and Linda clapped her hands together.

"They're lovely."

Cole knelt before her and held out the flowers for her to smell. "You look much better. How'd they treat you?"

Caroline hovered over Cole's back, holding her breath. If Linda told him about her suspicions, he might start looking at her again. She couldn't afford to have Cole prying into her past.

"Just fine. I feel better." Linda touched the petal of a pink rose. "Caroline, could you please put these in a vase for me? There's one in the cabinet beside the dining table."

"Of course." She held out a hand that was not altogether steady to take the flowers from Cole. "Do you want a cup of tea?"

Shaking his head, he perched on the arm of Linda's chair.

As she arranged the flowers in a vase, Linda and Cole exchanged small talk, but she didn't once hear the word *poison*.

Then Linda raised her voice. "Did Caroline tell you she's thinking of leaving town?"

The teakettle's piercing whistle interrupted Cole's response. Why did Linda have to keep up her matchmaking efforts? Caroline poured the boiling water over tea bags in the cups and carried them into the other room.

"I mentioned it to Cole last night," she said.

"I'm not sure small-town life suits Caroline." Cole raised his eyebrows at her, and she felt like sinking into bed and pulling the covers over her head.

There were so many lies swirling among the three of them right now, she couldn't keep them straight.

She sat down, cupping her warm mug. "Visiting family in Timberline has been a welcome respite, but I really need to start thinking about my future."

"And what does the future look like for Caroline… Johnson?"

Swallowing, she rolled her lips inward. Did he doubt her name now?

"One thing it includes is continued therapy, which I think is a wonderful plan." Linda blew on the surface of her tea and took a sip.

"I think it's a good plan, too. I saw a therapist a few times after my divorce, and it helped me," Cole admitted.

"Caroline has one more appointment with Dr. Shipman tomorrow before she leaves." Linda's gaze slid from Caroline's face to his. "In fact, I was wondering if you could take her to the appointment."

Caroline rolled her eyes at Cole and shook her head. "I thought I was going to borrow your car, Linda. You'll be having dinner with your girlfriends, right?"

"Yes, but your appointment is late and by the time you finish and drive back here, it'll be dark. I just don't think it's a wise idea for you to be on your own right now, Caroline, especially after a therapy appointment."

"It's therapy, not surgery. Besides, Cole probably doesn't want to drive me. I'll be fine."

"I have no problem driving you, and I happen to agree with Linda. Consider it a date." He leaned over and kissed Linda's cheek. "Now I have to get going. I have some research to do this afternoon."

"I'll walk you out to your car," Caroline said.

"Thank you for the flowers, Cole."

Caroline walked with him to the front door, her hand on his back, her knuckle drilling into his spine.

When they stepped onto the porch, he broke away. "Ouch. Why are you hustling me out of the house?"

Grabbing his hand, she dragged him into the driveway. "I thought you were going to say something about the man with the knife. I don't want Linda to know about that. She's had enough upset."

"Oh, is that why you don't want to tell her? You haven't reported it to the cops yet, either, have you?"

"No, and I'm not going to, which is a good thing for you, Mr. Rogue DEA Agent. What are you even doing here? What are you looking for?"

"You have your secrets, I have mine. I'm not going to tell you my business, but I will give you a ride tomorrow. You have someone running around town pulling knives on you, you haven't reported him to the police and you're going to drive off to Port Angeles by yourself? You're either brave, a martial arts expert or you know more about the knife attack than you're saying, which is no surprise. You know a lot more about a lot of things than you're saying."

She tossed her head, shaking her hair out of her face. "I will accept your ride, but I will not be cross-examined. Linda is still hoping for some kind of happily-ever-after for us."

"Ain't gonna happen." He snorted.

"You got that right." Somehow Caroline's gaze had dropped from his incredible green eyes to his incredible lips, and the sneer she'd planned for her own lips had softened into a pout.

He moved a step closer to her and she leaned in like a magnet. Cupping her face with one large hand, he possessed her mouth with a kiss so hot the drops of rain that had started falling sizzled on her skin.

He deepened his kiss and they stood locked together as the heavens opened above them. Without missing a beat, Cole flipped up the hood of his jacket and pulled it over both their heads.

She pulled away first, only because she'd lost feeling in the hands that had been gripping the sides of his jacket.

Resting his forehead against hers, nose to nose, he whispered, "No happily-ever-after here."

She tipped her head back, letting the rain course down her face, mingling with her tears. "Not for us."

As he reached for her again, she spun around and ran back to Linda's house. She slammed the front door behind her and leaned against it, panting.

"What took you so long? What were you doing out in the rain?"

"Saying goodbye."

CAROLINE STAYED INDOORS the following day. She spent most of her time at Linda's, watching TV, making sure

Linda was drinking lots of fluids, and trying not to think about Cole. She'd offered to open the store today, but Linda preferred her company here.

The afternoon rolled around quickly, and she went home to get ready for her appointment. She returned to Linda's with a coupon for the local pizza place. She waved it in the air. "You ladies are ordering pizza tonight, right? This coupon will get you a discount. It was with an advertisement on my doorknob."

"Leave it by the telephone." Linda sat up from where she'd been reclining on the sofa. "I'm feeling so much better now, and I want you to forget about what I said about being poisoned. I drank too much and got sick. End of story."

"That still doesn't change the fact that I need to be on my way. I need to start making some plans."

"You could do that here in Timberline."

"I don't think so." She sat next to Linda and took her hand. "While this place has felt like home, due mostly to your hospitality, there's something about it that's hostile. I feel the undercurrent."

"I understand. It's beautiful country, but the rain and the brooding forest aren't for everyone." The older woman squeezed Caroline's fingers. "Just take care of yourself wherever you land. Do not go back to Larry no matter what he promises, and drop me a line to let me know you're okay."

"You're wonderful." She blinked back a few tears. If her family had been anything like Linda Gunderson, she probably wouldn't be in this mess right now. What had she been running from? What brought her into Johnny Diamond's sphere?

She heard tires in the driveway and jumped up. "I'm going to run out there so Cole doesn't have to go into the rain, because you know he'll come right up to the door to get me."

"That's because he's a gentleman. And I know it won't be Cole you wind up with, but next time it should be someone like him."

"It will. I promise." She blew Linda a kiss before dashing down the driveway as Cole opened the car door.

She burst in the passenger side and shut the door on the rain. "You don't need to go out in that stuff."

"I think the storm is finally moving through. It might actually clear up by the time we get to Port Angeles."

"Are you going to do more *research* there, or what?"

"I have a few sources to check, but I'm getting to the end of the line. I didn't discover what I'd hoped to discover, and I actually want to take a real vacation for a week or so before I get back to work."

"Hawaii? Caribbean?"

"Nothing that exotic. I'm going to visit my sister and her family. They live in San Diego, too, but I'm not always in town."

"I'm sure it will be more relaxing than this."

"Yeah, I'm not one for relaxing."

"Since you're working on your time off, I guess not."

"Do you know where you're headed?" He held up one finger. "I'm not giving you the third degree."

"I think I'm going to get lost in a big city. I don't think small-town life is for me."

"Probably not. Everyone wants to know your business."

They switched to less loaded topics on the rest of the drive, and she discovered Cole played bass in an oldies cover band and had gone to college on a swimming scholarship.

His face lit up as he told her his stories, and she ached to tell him stories of her own, but she had nothing. Just a blank slate.

Laughing at Cole's account of a drunk at a bar trying to sing onstage with his band, she turned her head to look out the window. As they passed the Quileute reservation, an electric jolt seemed to pass through her body and she grabbed the edges of her seat.

"Something wrong?"

"I don't know." She massaged her temples. "It's like I just had a rush of adrenaline."

"Probably stress, that whole fight-or-flight thing. You probably need to release some steam, exercise. When I get that way, I need to hit the pool and do some laps. What do you like to do, run? You look like a runner."

"I am—long distances." Her heart tripped over itself. Where had that come from? It was the truth. She felt it. She was a runner. Maybe that had just come from seeing running clothes—shoes and shorts—in the suitcase from her former life. But it felt right. Just like the desert had felt right.

She repeated with a firm voice, "Yes, I'm a runner."

"I hate running, unless I'm chasing a suspect. Then I can get into it."

She liked to run, she preferred the desert and the Quileute reservation had given her a shock. She tapped on the glass of the window. "Did you mention that the man who kidnapped those children all those years ago was from the Quileute tribe?"

"Rocky Whitecotton? Yeah, although the tribe had pretty much disowned him even before they discovered he was behind the kidnappings. He didn't actually kidnap those kids himself. He had members of the Lords of Chaos do his dirty work." Cole shot her a sideways glance. "Why do you ask?"

"I saw the sign for the reservation back there. It reminded me of that guy."

"A real weirdo from what I've read."

"Do you think he killed those kids?"

Cole's jaw tightened and she remembered he liked kids. "Probably. No trace of them has ever been found."

She nodded and then started humming to the song on the radio. Why would Rocky Whitecotton be upset with Johnny Diamond for not finding her? What did she have to do with this whole drug trade?

Caroline felt primed for her session with Dr. Shipman and couldn't wait to get into that office.

She and Cole exchanged more small talk until they reached the coast and Port Angeles.

He pulled up to the curb in front of the office building. "An hour?"

"That should do it. I'll be out front at six."

"I'll be here. Have a good session."

As she opened the car door, a gust of wind snatched it from her grasp, flinging it open. "Sorry. I guess we have the wind to thank for blowing the clouds away, though."

Ducking her head against the strong breeze, she ran toward the low-slung stucco building. She grabbed the handle of Dr. Shipman's door and pulled it open, careful to keep a grip on it as the wind blasted through the open spaces of the office building.

She clicked it behind her and smoothed her hair back. The door to Dr. Shipman's office remained firmly closed, so Caroline pushed the button on the wall to indicate her presence.

She picked up a magazine and thumbed through it while bracing her shoulder against one wall. A few pages later, when Dr. Shipman still hadn't opened her door, Caroline checked the time on her phone—five after five.

She was probably with another patient. Caroline dropped the magazine and glanced at her phone again. Should she text Cole and let him know she'd be running late?

She doubted he even had business in Port Angeles. He seemed ready to wrap up his fruitless investigation— fruitless because he'd located his quarry but hadn't realized it.

She tapped her toe as another ten minutes passed. Should she knock? Maybe another patient was having a breakthrough—or a breakdown. She took out her phone again and called Dr. Shipman.

Her phone rang twice and rolled over to voice mail. Jules must've turned it off for a session.

Caroline crept up to the inner-office door and pressed her ear against the solid wood, her hand falling to the doorknob. No voices murmured in the space beyond.

Had Dr. Shipman forgotten about the session? Caroline rapped lightly on the door and held her breath. She tried again. "Dr. Shipman? Jules?"

She flattened her palms against the door and licked her lips as a puff of fear lifted the hair on the back of her neck. It came out of nowhere, perhaps originating with the dead silence from the office.

Her fingers curled around the door handle again. This time she twisted—and it turned.

She bumped the door with her hip, opening it a crack. "Jules?"

The low light of the office indicated Dr. Shipman had been in session. Caroline eased the door open farther. The hushed atmosphere of the empty room repelled her and she recoiled.

Then a piece of paper caught her attention—and the single white square on the floor sent her pulse racing. She'd been in this office only once, but that had been enough to tell her that Dr. Shipman was precise and orderly. Why would she leave a piece of paper on the floor unless she'd departed in a hurry?

Caroline squared her shoulders and strode into the room. The air closed in around her, heavy and dank. She choked on a metallic odor that filled her nose and mouth.

She couldn't stop herself. She wanted to, but her legs wouldn't listen to her screaming brain. Crossing to the desk, her feet sank into the carpet with a slow, methodical pace.

She peered around the edge of the solid piece of furniture, her gaze tracking from the single low-heeled pump on its side to the dark, wet stain on the carpet, to Dr. Shipman's blank stare.

And then the memories hit her.

Chapter Eleven

The wind picked up the leaves on the walkway and stirred them into a mini tornado. Digging his elbows into his knees, Cole balanced his chin on his clasped hands.

If Caroline wasn't running some kind of scam, why didn't she trust him enough to tell him what was going on with her? Maybe he could even help.

For everything he'd learned from his sister about letting his sensitive side show with women, he must be failing miserably. Caroline was as secretive now as the day he'd met her in the library. Of course, that had been only a few days ago, even though it seemed as if he'd known her a lot longer.

He sat back and took a sip of his coffee. He didn't have any investigating to do in Port Angeles, and Caroline had probably already figured that out. So, after he picked up a coffee, he decided to wait for her on a bench outside the office, even though he'd be sitting here for another forty minutes.

A low wail started somewhere in the building before he heard a door crash open. He jumped up from the cement bench in time to see Caroline flying out one of the offices, her mouth open as she struggled with a scream.

The scream finally won, and the high-pitched sound sent a river of chills down his spine. He rushed toward her, and she blindly fought him off, scratching and kicking, until her wide blue eyes locked on to his and she collapsed against his chest.

"My God. What happened? What happened in there?" He started to move toward the open door, becoming aware of a few people poking their heads outside, but Caroline hung on to him, dragging him away.

"Caroline, what's wrong?"

"She's dead. Dr. Shipman is dead. Someone slit her throat."

A spike of adrenaline shot through him. "Are you sure?"

"I don't know. I don't know. Don't make me go back."

A man hung over the iron railing on the second floor of the building and called down, "Should I phone 911?"

"Yes." Cole glanced at Caroline. "Possible dead body."

Caroline sobbed and sagged against his chest. He stroked her soft hair. "Can you wait here? I want to take a look myself."

She grabbed his shirt. "Do you think I don't know what a dead body looks like? I know."

A few other tenants from the building gathered outside, and a woman spoke up. "Is it Dr. Shipman?"

"Yes, did you see anything? Hear anything?" Cole asked.

The woman called back, "I didn't see or hear a thing. I didn't hear any gunfire. Was there gunfire?"

Cole led Caroline to the bench he'd just vacated in a hurry and urged her to sit. Crouching in front of her and taking her hands, he said, "Can you wait here while I have a look?"

"I'll stay with her." The woman who had spoken before turned and locked her office door. "The police should be here any minute."

"Is that okay with you?" He touched Caroline's pale cheek and she nodded, her eyes still seeing something far, far away.

Cole lunged to his feet and walked up to the yawning door of Dr. Shipman's office. He crept into the outer office, where nothing seemed out of place, and proceeded to the open door of the inner office.

He poked his head in first and sniffed, detecting the odor of blood. She must've lost a lot to have the smell permeate the air.

Keeping his hands to himself, he crept farther into the office, noting a piece of paper on the floor, but nothing else amiss. When he got to the heavy oak desk, he peered over the top.

A woman, presumably Dr. Shipman, lay sprawled on the floor, one arm out to her side, the other flung across her waist. She'd probably been dead or well on her way by the time she hit the floor.

A gash marred the slim column of her throat, and blood soaked the gray carpet beneath her head and neck. Cole scanned the floor for the murder weapon, but just that single piece of paper stood out.

The items on her desk were well-ordered and upright. Dr. Shipman had been caught off guard, with no time to put up a fight. His gaze swept the area and he detected small specks of blood on the door behind the desk. It must be spray from the initial cut, when the knife sliced through her artery.

The killer hadn't escaped that shower of blood, even standing behind Dr. Shipman, which he must've been doing. He never would've been able to stroll out the front of the office.

Cole pinned his gaze on the back door, which must lead to a parking lot or alley. The perp had probably sneaked out through there.

The sirens rolling up outside disturbed Cole's concentration, and he closed his eyes and took a deep breath. Why would someone want to kill Caroline's therapist? He had no doubt in his mind that Dr. Shipman's death was related to the craziness swirling around Caroline.

He heard voices at the office door. "Hello? This is the police. Come out with your hands up."

He turned away from the body and walked into the waiting room with his hands held clearly in front of him. "I'm Cole Pierson, a friend of the woman who found the body. I'm also a DEA agent."

The Port Angeles police officer leading the charge kept his weapon aloft. "Anyone else in there?"

"Just the dead body—Dr. Shipman, throat slashed."

The other officer stepped around his partner. "Do you have some ID?"

Cole spread apart his fingers. "In the right inside pocket of my jacket. My weapon's in my left jacket pocket."

The cop responded, "Let's see your identification."

Cole carefully pulled out his DEA badge and handed it over.

The officer glanced at it and holstered his gun. "Were you with Ms. Johnson when she found the body?"

"No, I was waiting outside to pick her up, when she left the office, screaming."

"Why'd you come inside?"

The other police officer had started moving toward the inner office.

"I just wanted to see if Dr. Shipman needed assistance."

"Did she?"

"Already dead, throat slit." Cole slid his badge back into his pocket. "I didn't touch anything in here, but my friend may have."

"We have two homicide detectives from Clallam County on the way, so we'll let them do the heavy lifting. We're here to secure the crime scene."

Cole backed out of the office. "I'll let you get to work. There's a back door in that office. The killer probably made his way out through that door."

When he stepped outside, Cole gulped in buckets of fresh air and headed toward Caroline, still on the bench with an officer talking to her.

She glanced up at his approach, her eyes glassy and vacant.

He caught the tail end of their conversation. "I—I don't have any ID. I lost my wallet on the way to Timberline. I haven't had time to replace my driver's license…or anything else."

Cole flipped his badge open for the officer. "Is there a problem?"

Eyeing Cole's badge, the cop said, "I asked Ms. Johnson for her driver's license or ID, and she doesn't have any."

"Yeah, she lost her wallet last week." Cole avoided the wide-eyed stare Caroline turned on him.

The officer frowned and tapped his pencil. "Can you vouch for her?"

"Sure."

"I'll need your cell phone number, Ms. Johnson. We're going to have to verify your identity."

She gave him the number and he wrote it down. "Do not leave the area. You're a witness, and like I said, we're going to have to verify your identity. Thanks to Agent Pierson, I'm not taking you in now to fingerprint you, but you'll have to come to the station tomorrow for an interview and we'll do it then."

"Okay, thank you. I'll be there."

"That's all I have, but the homicide detectives from county will want to question you when they arrive."

"All right, but I told you everything I know. I had an appointment with Dr. Shipman, buzzed her when I walked in, called her and then listened at her door. When I didn't hear any voices, I opened the door and... found her body." Caroline rubbed her nose. "I didn't know her well. I had seen her only once before."

"Okay, well, you can repeat all of that to the detectives. Please wait here for a few more minutes."

The officer talked briefly to Cole and then started clearing curious looky-loos away from the office door.

Cole sat down next to her and stretched his legs in front of him. "What's going on, Caroline?"

She jerked her head toward him. "I don't know. Why are you asking me that?"

He lowered his voice. "You know why Dr. Shipman was murdered."

"Why would you say that? I barely knew her. One session—that's all we had."

"What did you tell her in that one session that someone didn't want her to know?"

"I don't know what you're talking about." Her face crumpled and she covered it with both hands—hiding her lying lips, her lying eyes.

A man in a black suit and dark red tie approached them. "Ms. Johnson? I'm Detective Rowan with the Clallam County Homicide Department. I understand you found Dr. Shipman's body."

She dropped her hands. "I did."

"Can you tell me the circumstances of your visit and what happened?"

Caroline repeated her story, never veering from what she'd told the Port Angeles police officer.

Detective Rowan had a few questions for Cole, too, and then took their phone numbers before heading for the cops clustered around the doorway of Dr. Shipman's office.

"That's your story and you're sticking to it? You're a one-time patient of Dr. Shipman's in the wrong place at the wrong time?" Cole murmured.

"What do you want from me?"

"How about the truth?"

She gripped his arm, her fingernails digging into him through the sleeve of his jacket. "I didn't kill anyone."

He blinked. "I never accused you of killing Dr. Shipman or anyone else. I doubt you have the strength to come up behind someone and slit their throat, although Dr. Shipman looked petite, like you. That's why a lot of women choose poison as their murder weapon of choice."

Caroline's face drained of all color and her eye twitched.

All the noise and activity around Cole ceased, replaced by a roaring in his ears. It had been right in front of him all along—a petite woman with a black cap heading to Timberline. His first instincts had been correct, but her relationship to Linda Gunderson had thrown him off. Had a sweet lady like Linda been lying all this time? Why would she lie for a complete stranger? Unless they really were cousins and that's why Caroline was on her way to Timberline.

Caroline half rose from the bench and Cole grabbed her arm and pulled her back down. "Poison. What do you know about poison?"

Her jaw hardened. "Nothing. I don't know what you're talking about. I didn't kill anyone. I know that now."

"Now? You know that *now*?"

She glanced at the huddle of cops. "Shh."

"You're going to tell me what's going on, Caroline Johnson, and you're going to tell me now." His fingers still encircled her wrist in a vise and he became aware of the delicacy of her bones. He loosened his hold. "You can't go on like this."

"I know." She rubbed her palms against the denim covering her thighs. "But not here."

She stood up and swayed, and he jumped up next to her and caught her arm. "Drink?"

She nodded.

Taking her arm lightly, he checked in with the detective and then led her across the street to his rental car, which it seemed he'd parked there days ago.

When Caroline had snapped her seat belt, she turned to him. "What were you doing at the office so early?"

He cranked on the ignition. Were they both telling the truth now? "I didn't have any research to do. What I'd been looking for had been right under my nose all along, and I didn't see it because…"

"Because?"

"I didn't want to." He threw the car into Drive and squealed away from the curb.

He found a restaurant overlooking the harbor, and they bypassed the dining area and headed straight for the bar. As one couple rose to leave a table in the corner by the window, Cole claimed it.

A busboy scurried over and collected the glasses and wiped the table. "A waitress will be right with you, or you can order at the bar and bring it back to the table."

"We'll wait." Cole pulled out a chair and sat down like he was ready to conduct an interrogation. He was.

Before he could start with his first question, the waitress was taking their drink order.

When she left, Cole hunched forward. "Who the hell are you?"

"Let me tell this my way. I'm not going to be bullied."

"Me? A bully? I think I'm handling you with kid gloves considering you've been lying to me from day one and playing me for a fool."

"Playing you for a fool? I hardly think that's the case."

"Really?" His hands curled into fists. "The longing looks. The gentle touches. The kisses."

She made a cross with her two index fingers. "Whoa. *You* kissed *me*."

The waitress cleared her throat. "One chardonnay and an Angeles IPA on tap."

She left them to their private conversation, and Cole straightened the edge of the cocktail napkin beneath his beer mug. He had to get a grip, put his bruised ego aside and focus on the important issues at hand. "Go for it."

Caroline splayed her hands on the table and her chest rose and fell quickly. "I'm the person you're looking for. I was in that room with Johnny Diamond when he died."

A muscle twitched at the corner of Cole's mouth. She'd been right under his nose all this time. Once again he'd allowed his attraction to someone to derail his instincts and common sense.

He gulped back some beer and wrapped his hands around the mug, squeezing until his knuckles were white. He returned to the one piece of information that had thrown him off. "Are you related to Linda Gunderson?"

"No. I'd never seen her before in my life, or at least

not that I know of." Caroline's lips tilted up on one side in a half smile.

"I'm glad you think this is amusing. How'd you con her? How'd you get her to lie for you—and so convincingly?"

"When she first saw me in Timberline, she thought I was a battered woman." Caroline touched the fading, yellow bruise on her right cheekbone. "Her sister had been abused by a boyfriend, and she was very sensitive to that. I'm ashamed to admit it, but I did play on that. I told her a story about Larry and how I'd escaped from him and wanted to remain undercover. She's the one who suggested the family connection."

"Wow. So, how close did you stay to the truth? Were you Diamond's woman?" Cole had to take another sip of beer to wash the bitterness of that statement from his mouth. "Did he knock you around…before you poisoned him?"

A splash of wine hit the table as her hand jerked. "I told you. I didn't kill anyone, and that includes Johnny Diamond. After I discovered Dr. Shipman's body, I remembered everything that happened in that room at the Stardust Motel."

Cole's nostrils flared as he narrowed his eyes. "You remember what happened? I would hope so."

She licked a drop of wine from her lips. "But that's all I remember. I don't remember what happened before that."

"What are you talking about?" The antennae that had been suppressed by his feelings for Caroline began to wake up and get ready for another snow job. "Who the hell are you and what's your connection to Diamond?"

"I—I don't know."

"Is that why you were seeing Dr. Shipman, to find yourself? That's all very new age, but—" he drilled his finger into the tabletop "—I want answers right now. Who are you?"

"I told you. I don't know." She smacked the table with her palm. "I have amnesia. I don't know who I am."

Cole opened his mouth. Closed it. Ran a hand through his hair. Took a long pull from his glass.

What the hell could you say to that?

Chapter Twelve

Cole's jaw tightened and then he ground out, "You're lying."

She grabbed his hand. "I'm not lying, Cole. I don't know who I am."

He left his hand beneath hers, cold and unresponsive—just like his hard green eyes.

Once she knew for sure she hadn't killed Diamond, she'd wanted to confess everything to Cole, or at least everything she remembered. She couldn't carry this burden by herself anymore, but she hoped she hadn't made a mistake trusting Cole.

"Why didn't you go straight to the police? They could fingerprint you, just like they're going to do tomorrow. They could tell you like *that*—" he snapped his fingers "—who you are. Even if you're not a criminal, you might have a thumbprint on file for a driver's license or any kind of background check."

"I was afraid. I woke up in a seedy motel room with a dead man. There had obviously been a struggle. I found cash and drugs in the room and the body of a dead woman in the trunk of the car. I had no memory of what I was doing there, who I was." Caroline's bottom lip trembled and she sucked it between her teeth. She wanted Cole to believe her because she told a convincing story, not because he felt sorry for her.

"I didn't know if I had murdered someone, was involved in the drug trade or had pissed off someone in the drug trade. I was afraid if I'd gone to the cops, they'd arrest me."

"You said you remembered what happened at the Stardust. So, what happened?" Cole folded his arms across his chest, which looked huge and implacable right now.

"Johnny was going to kill me or at least incapacitate me with some drug. He thought I was in the bathroom, taking a shower, but I was looking for an opportunity to escape. I cracked open the bathroom door and saw him mixing up some powder in a bottle of water. I knew he was going to suggest I drink the water, so when I came out of the bathroom I swapped the poisoned bottle with another one in the mini fridge. He had no idea I'd seen him put the poison in the water bottle, so when he went out to the car I switched the bottles. When he returned to the room, I made sure he saw me drink the water he thought was poisoned."

"He drank the poisoned water from the fridge later?"

"Yes. He kept watching me for signs of the poison. If I had been smart I would've pretended to feel the effects, but then *he* started to feel the effects. He knew right away what I'd done, but it was too late. That's when I got the bruise on my face and the head injury that would cause my amnesia."

"He attacked you?"

"When he realized what I had done, he punched me and threw me across the room. I think he would've killed me with his bare hands if the poison hadn't started doing a number on his system. I never saw the end of him, since I'd lost consciousness by the time he died."

Cole blew out a breath. "That's quite a story, but a lot of questions remain. What were you doing with him in the first place and why was he trying to kill you?"

"That I can't tell you." She took a sip of wine and relaxed into the warmth that spread through her body. Cole might not believe her yet, but she felt as if she'd just shrugged a hundred pounds of weight off her shoulders.

"When I discovered Dr. Shipman's body, all those memories from the motel room flooded my mind. The whole scene played out in my head like a movie."

He rubbed his chin. "Why would Diamond use poison to kill you? Why not strangle you like he did Hazel McTavish?"

"The woman in the trunk."

"Maybe he was just trying to incapacitate you and not kill you." Cole drew a pattern on the tabletop with his finger as if he were connecting dots. "But the dose he was planning for you killed him, and he was a big man. Unless…"

"What?" She leaned forward, lips parted.

"Unless he didn't plan to allow you to drink all the water. If a few sips had knocked you out, he could've taken the bottle or knocked it over."

She nodded. "That could be. Anyway, when I woke up in that condition, I couldn't remember any of that. When I found Hazel's body in the trunk of her car, I knew I had to get away. I took the suitcase that was obviously mine and a little cash from the bag in the room, which I swear I'll pay back, and took off for Timberline."

"Why Timberline?"

She reached into her purse, hanging from the back of her chair, and withdrew the slip of paper. She smoothed it out on the table in front of Cole. "This was in my jacket pocket. I figured maybe I had people here, friends, someone who could help me out."

He pinched a corner of the paper between two fingers. "Probably not the smartest move, as Diamond's associates could trace you to Timberline…and probably did."

"Why would they?" She pressed a hand against her pounding heart. "This paper was in *my* pocket, in *my* handwriting. I tested that. I always figured Johnny waylaid me on my way to Timberline."

"Caroline, didn't you ever wonder how I tracked you to Timberline?"

Heat splashed her cheeks. "I—I thought maybe because Johnny had connections to the area. I searched for the story of his murder when I got to town. That's how I discovered his name. I thought that's maybe why you were looking here first, and of course, I didn't know you were DEA when we first met. How did you know to come to Timberline? And how did you know to look for a woman?"

"Someone had entered Timberline in the GPS of Hazel's car, and someone saw you leave the motel room that morning."

She sucked in a quick breath. "Who?"

"A maid at the motel. But you disguised yourself well. All she could tell me was a petite woman with a dark beanie had been near the car that morning."

Caroline massaged the back of her neck. "I feel pretty stupid. I don't know how I thought I could outwit the police or a bunch of drug dealers."

"You've done a good job of it so far. Linda was the key. When she spoke so glowingly of her cousin, it made me doubt I'd found my woman."

Heat crept up Caroline's throat at his phrasing and she dropped her gaze to the table. "I'm glad you did find me, Cole. C-can you help me now? I'm afraid I've endangered Linda's life, too. When she got sick the other night, she thought she might've been poisoned. I think I was the intended target, but I'm afraid for her."

She put her hand over her heart. "I swear to you, I didn't kill Johnny. It happened just the way I told you. I'm afraid the man in the driveway the other night is one of Johnny's guys, although I don't know how they know I'm here or why they suspect I have any money."

Cole cleared his throat. "We let that slip out, Caroline. We have informants, moles in the drug community, and we let it be known that copious amounts of cash had been stolen from Diamond's stash."

She covered her mouth. "They think I have it, but who am I? Why was I traveling with Johnny?"

"Maybe once we confirm your identity, we'll have the answer to that."

"I read in an online news story that Johnny carjacked and murdered Hazel McTavish from a parking lot at the Sea-Tac Airport to get her car. Who's to say he didn't do the same to me? Maybe I was just at that hotel or maybe I was riding in Hazel's car."

Caroline raised her brows at Cole, hoping for confirmation, reassurance.

Scratching his stubble, he said, "You had a piece of paper with Timberline written on it. Also, why would Johnny want to poison a complete stranger? As much as I want you and Johnny Diamond to be strangers, I just can't see it."

She collapsed against the back of her chair. "I know we weren't strangers."

"Did you remember something else?"

"It's not something I just remembered. It's something I knew all along." She smoothed her hands across her face. "Did you wonder why Johnny didn't have a cell phone with him?"

"You took it?"

"I was afraid he might have my name, number or picture on it. Since I didn't know my name, I wouldn't have been able to tell."

"What did you do with the phone?"

"Took out the battery and the SIM card, destroyed the phone and dumped it on the side of the highway—but not before I read an incoming text."

"What did it say?"

"It said 'Did you get the girl? Rocky's…' and then it had a little devil emoticon."

Cole's eyebrows collided over his nose. "Rocky?"

"Rocky. Timberline. What are the odds?" She tossed back the rest of her wine. "Not only am I connected to Johnny Diamond in some way, I'm also connected to Rocky Whitecotton, a man who kidnapped and probably murdered three children."

"This is a great clue, Caroline. I'm gonna phone it in to my partner, see if he can look up some connection between Johnny Diamond and Rocky Whitecotton."

"I'm glad I could do something to help, since all I've been doing is putting up roadblocks for you and the DEA."

Cole ran a hand across his mouth. "I know I'm stating the obvious here, but you need to find out who you are."

Her pulse quickened and a flash of joy shot through her body. "Does that mean you believe me?"

"I may be crazy or just blinded by…my feelings, but that's a wild story for anyone to concoct. Not to mention, if you were working with Johnny Diamond and Rocky Whitecotton, you wouldn't be in Timberline fraternizing with the DEA."

"Is that what this is?" She picked up her wineglass and swirled the drop of golden liquid in the bottom. "Fraternizing?"

Cole grunted and signaled to the waitress for another round. "Of course, there's always the possibility that you *are* in league with those two and you just don't remember. Have you remembered anything since coming to Timberline?"

"It's not exactly a memory, but I can understand and speak Spanish. I discovered that while stumbling across a Spanish language TV show."

"God, it's so strange how the mind works. What did you recall during that first session with Dr. Shipman?"

Caroline raised a hand to her throat as memories of Dr. Shipman's body and the lurid gash leaking her blood onto the floor slammed into her full force. "She hypnotized me. I remembered being part of a large family somewhere in the desert, but I was desperate to leave."

"Maybe you did leave and Diamond was sent to bring you back."

"To whom? To what? What kind of family sends drug traffickers to retrieve their family members?"

"A crazy one—plenty of those out there." Cole smiled at the waitress as she brought their drinks, and as soon as she turned her back, his face resumed its serious expression. "You started to remember with Dr. Shipman and you may have continued your progress today, but someone made sure that didn't happen by taking out Shipman."

"I thought of that." Caroline curled up the edge of her cocktail napkin with fidgeting fingers.

"That means whoever is watching you, whether it's the guy with the knife or someone else, suspects you've lost your memory and knows you've been seeing Dr. Shipman to get it back."

"How could he know I was seeing Dr. Shipman? How would he know I had an appointment today? Because I don't think it's a coincidence I'm the one who found her."

Cole froze. Then he closed his eyes and cursed. "If they're watching you, they know you've been with me. I'm the one with the car."

"You mean they've been following you? Following us?"

"Worse. I probably would've picked up a tail…but not a bug."

"A bug, like a tracking device?"

He jerked his thumb over his shoulder. "They probably know we're sitting in this restaurant right now."

A sudden chill claimed her body and she dropped her hand from her wineglass to her lap. "They've been tracking our movements?"

"My guess is Linda's car also has a bug."

"I think I might know who it is."

"But you didn't even see the man with the knife in the driveway."

"Not him, although he's probably part of the team. A man came into Timberline Treasures the other day, and I got a weird vibe from him. I've seen him a few times since." Caroline lifted her shoulders. "I even did a little sleuthing myself."

"You followed him?"

"I saw him talking to a local Realtor in Sutter's, and I paid a visit to her—Rebecca Geist. I couldn't get much out of her. I pretended he looked familiar to me, but she was closemouthed about him."

"What does he look like?"

"Medium height, shaved head, around thirty. Nice-looking guy. Looks more like a software engineer for Evergreen than a drug dealer."

"You never know. I've seen all kinds. I'll have a look at him. First—" he rapped his knuckles on the table, making the wine in her glass dance "—we need to find out who you are. The fastest way is to bring you by the Port Angeles Police Station tomorrow and get you fingerprinted."

"I'm scared." She stuffed her hands beneath her thighs. "What if I'm someone…bad?"

"We'll deal with it, Caroline. Whatever happens, we'll deal with it. You need to be protected one way or the other."

One side of her mouth quirked up. "I thought that's what you were doing."

"I can do it a lot better if I know who you are and what your role is in all this."

Her gaze dropped to the full glass of wine the waitress had put before her. "And if it turns out I'm one of the bad guys? Will you arrest me?"

"We're a long way from that right now." Cole wedged a finger beneath her chin and tilted up her head. "Do you trust me?"

"I have to. You're all I have."

He pulled some cash from his pocket. "Are you going to finish that wine?"

"No."

"Then let's get out of here and take care of that bug."

When they got to the parking lot, she stood aside and watched as Cole slid beneath his rental car with his legs sticking out.

Several minutes later, he emerged with a broad smile on his face and a black object in his greasy palm. "Got the little son of a bitch."

Seeing the bug in his hand gave her a shock, even though Cole had been confident it was there. Despite what the man with the knife and Dr. Shipman's murder indicated, the tracking device was solid proof someone in Timberline had her in his sights.

Could she put her faith in Cole or would it better to run? She could put everyone and everything behind her and continue with her plan of melting into a big city until she knew for sure who she was and if she'd committed any crimes.

Of course, she was a day away from the fingerprints that would tell her all she needed to know.

Cole obliterated the bug beneath the heel of his boot and then swept the pieces into the water. "I'll do the same to the one on Linda's car. Let's get out of here."

Caroline took a step away from the vehicle, twisting her fingers in front of her. "Where are we going? A-are you going to turn me in?"

"Turn you in? You don't trust me, do you?" He opened the passenger door and made a sweeping motion with his hand. "I'm not going to turn you in, Caroline. I'm not even officially on duty. We'll see what happens with the fingerprints tomorrow, but you have to promise me you won't bolt."

Had he read her mind? "What happens if the fingerprints tell you I'm a wanted criminal? A drug dealer?"

"I doubt that's going to happen. If it does, I can at

least remand you to psychiatric care. Nobody's going to toss you into prison."

Psychiatric care? She didn't much like the sound of that, either, but what choice did she have unless she planned to make a run for it tonight?

And that was not out of the realm of possibility.

Chapter Thirteen

Neither of them had been able to eat a thing at the restaurant in Port Angeles, so by the time they reached Timberline, they were both starving.

As Cole drove up to the duplex, Caroline asked, "Should I tell Linda what happened?"

"She probably heard it on the news by now, anyway."

"But the police won't release my name, will they?"

"They're not releasing your name. I asked them not to, and the press wasn't there yet when we left."

"Thank you." She touched his forearm, tense and corded. "Thanks for protecting me. I know if you hadn't been there or hadn't vouched for me, the cops would've taken me in."

He rolled into the driveway and parked. "Don't be too grateful. I didn't want to turn you over to the system just yet. We'll want first crack at you."

"Well, thanks, anyway." She popped open the door. "I'll deal with Linda. Should I tell her the jig is up?"

"Tell her what you like, but you're not doing it alone." He turned off the engine. "I'm not letting you out of my sight."

Her stomach knotted and she tried to swallow against her tight throat. Even if she wanted to bolt, Cole wouldn't let her.

She shrugged. "Suit yourself."

She slammed the car door and stalked up to Linda's porch with Cole literally on her tail.

He grabbed her arm. "Hold on. Shine your phone light beneath Linda's car for me, so I can search for that bug."

She obliged, and just like in the parking lot of the restaurant in Port Angeles, Cole emerged with the same type of device he'd found on his car. He destroyed it and pocketed the evidence.

"We're not telling Linda about that." She stepped onto the porch and knocked once. "Linda? It's Caroline… and Cole."

There was no answer above the murmur of the TV, and Caroline's already frazzled nerves unraveled a little more. "Linda?"

"I'll be right there."

Relief flooded Caroline's body, so fast and strong she had to brace a hand against the doorjamb to steady herself.

A minute later, Linda opened the door. "Are you all right? I heard about the murder of Dr. Shipman, and I've been worried sick about you."

"It was terrible." Caroline gave the older woman a quick hug. "The police were at her office when we got there."

"Oh, such a shame, and when you were late coming back…" Linda pressed a hand over her heart.

"Caroline needed a drink after the news—we both did."

"I'm glad Cole was with you." Linda clung to Caroline's arm. "Do the police have any idea who did it? A current patient?"

"They didn't tell us anything, and of course, I'd seen her only once."

Linda clicked her tongue. "Such horrible news and too close for comfort."

"Are you feeling better, Linda?" Caroline glanced around the tidy living room. "Did your friends drop by?"

"I'm fine. Everyone made such a fuss, but they did bring goodies and they cleaned up everything before they left. I'm going to get into bed early and read."

"That sounds like a good idea. We'll be right next door if you need anything."

"You and Cole?" Linda's eyes kindled with that matchmaking light.

"Neither one of us had dinner, so we'll probably order in some pizza."

"I wish I had some leftovers to give you, but we ate all our pizza. Would you like to take some brownies for dessert?" Linda bustled to the kitchen with that familiar spring to her step. "Karen made a double batch of her famous brownies and then had the nerve to leave them all here."

"Homemade brownies sound like the cure for everything right now." Cole joined her in the kitchen, and she handed him an oblong plastic container. "Are you sure you're going to be okay, Linda?"

"I'll be fine, especially knowing the two of you are next door." When she opened the door, she touched Caroline's cheek. "I'm so sorry about Dr. Shipman and that you had to be exposed to more violence. You need a nice, long vacation."

"I just might take one."

Cole's body stiffened beside her and she pushed past him on her way out the door.

He kept pace with her, balancing the plastic container full of brownies on one hand. "Pizza sounds good. How about a movie to go with it? I'm not tired. I can stay awake all night if I have to."

On her porch, she rounded on him. "Am I your prisoner now?"

"Better mine than the Clallam County Sheriff's Department."

She threw open her front door and dropped her purse on the kitchen table. She thrust her phone and the pizza advertisement that had been hanging on her doorknob earlier at him. "Anything but anchovies."

"And pineapple. I hate pineapple on my pizza."

He phoned in the order, while she pulled off her boots and turned up the thermostat. Maybe she could lull him to sleep with food, beer and heat.

"Do you want a beer?"

His eyes narrowed. "I'm good."

"Wine?"

"Don't drink the stuff, but you knock yourself out."

She stood at her open refrigerator door. "I think I'll have a diet soda instead."

"Caffeinated?"

"Yes."

"I'll have the same."

She stuffed down her irritation as she grabbed the sodas from the fridge. She didn't want him to think she resented the babysitting. Because if she let that show, he'd suspect that she had plans of running, not that she didn't. But the less she revealed her emotions to him, the better.

She rinsed the tops of the soda cans and wiped them with a paper towel. "Can okay?"

"Always tastes better from the can." He'd pulled off his own boots and now sat on her small sofa with his stocking feet propped up on the coffee table.

"Make yourself at home." She handed him the can and sat on the chair across from him—the only other place to sit in the living room.

"I will, thanks." He snapped the lid and slurped the foam from the top. "Did you shake this first so it would explode all over my shirt and I'd be forced to go back to my hotel and change?"

"Oh, stop. I'm not going anywhere. It's time I learn the truth—good or bad."

He hunched forward, resting his forearms on his knees, clasping his hands lightly. "Seriously, Caroline. It's for the best and for your own safety. The people after you killed Dr. Shipman. They're capable of anything."

"You're right. I think the only reason I've lasted this long is they probably figured out there's something wrong with me. I haven't done what they expected me to do. I haven't told anyone about Johnny. I've been pretending to be Linda's cousin." She massaged her temples. "Honestly, I don't know what they think. I didn't even take that much money from Johnny's bag. I just needed a little seed money, a head start."

"Do you want to give me that money now?"

She scooted forward in the chair. "Will that look good for me? If I hand over the money I took?"

"Anything will help."

She didn't want it, anyway. She launched herself out of the chair and headed for her bedroom, where she pulled up the rug in the closet. She felt for the uneven floorboard and pushed on one edge until the other side tipped up. She lifted the slat, ran her fingers along the stacks of bills and then collected them all. She replaced the board and the rug and returned to the living room.

"Here you go." She dumped the cash on the sofa cushion next to Cole.

Raising one eyebrow, he thumbed through the neat stacks. "This is not a small amount."

"I didn't know how much I'd need to get started somewhere else. I—I haven't used that much of it."

"Do you have a bag or something? I'd hate to stuff this much cash in my pockets—and I'd need some big pockets."

She pivoted toward the kitchen and pulled a cloth grocery bag from a drawer. "You can have this."

He took the sack dangling from her fingers and proceeded to tuck the stacks inside. "This will go over well."

The doorbell rang and they both twitched as if they expected someone had come for the money.

She crept to the window and peered out. "It's the pizza."

"I'll get it." Cole wedged the bag of money between the sofa and the end table and rose to his feet, reaching for his wallet.

After he paid for the pizza, he took it into the kitchen. "How many pieces?"

"I'll start with two and work my way up." Caroline peeled apart two paper plates that had come with the pizza and slapped them down on the counter.

Cole placed two pieces on one plate and three on another. They resumed their positions across from each other and ate for a while in silence.

Cole waved a piece of crust at her. "Have you ever tried to remember on your own?"

"All the time, until my brain hurt."

"Have you tried self-hypnosis or meditation?"

"Like swinging something in front of my own face and telling myself I'm getting sleepy?"

"A darkened room, a fixed object, silence, relaxation."

"Yeah, because I've had so much silence and time to relax since I've been on the run."

"It's coming back to you in flashes, though. The trauma of discovering Dr. Shipman's body prompted a break, didn't it?"

Caroline covered her mouth and closed her eyes, the horror of that moment creeping back into her psyche after she'd been pushing it aside all night. Dr. Shipman had mentioned in their first session that a trauma might start the flow of memories—she just hadn't known the trauma would be her own murder.

"What a terrible way to die. There was no struggle in that room. She must've known him—or thought she did."

"He could've been posing as a patient."

"I never saw any of her patients. Well, just one, a dark-skinned man with longish hair. I'm sure the police have tracked down all her clients." Caroline lunged for the remote. "Could we just watch a movie? Something mindless?"

"I'm all for mindless entertainment. What's on?"

"Linda and Louise have premium cable in here, so we should have lots of choices."

Caroline paused at a raunchy comedy about drug dealers, and Cole shook his head. "I don't think so."

She flipped through a few more shows and gestured to a romantic comedy. "Is this better?"

"This is one of my sister's favorite movies. I could really impress her and score points if I actually watched it. Do you want to watch it?"

"Romance *and* comedy? Just what I need." Caroline curled her feet beneath her in the straight-back chair.

"More pizza?" Cole held up his empty plate.

"Maybe later."

He pushed out of the sofa, took their paper plates and napkins to the kitchen and returned with one glass of wine. He patted the cushion next to him. "Why don't you come over here and get comfortable. You could use a glass of wine, too. You're still suffering from the shock of Dr. Shipman. I can see it in your eyes."

Her gaze darted from the sofa to the wine to his face. Caroline wanted all three more than anything right now. She uncurled her body from the chair and joined him.

Hell, she might be in jail by tomorrow night. Might as well live it up.

She cupped the wineglass in her hands. "Are you sure you don't want a glass or a beer?"

"After everything that's gone on today? I'd rather stay alert."

She eased back against the cushion, taking a sip of wine. It warmed her chest and belly and made her fingertips tingle. "Ahh."

"I thought so." Cole squeezed her knee. "Take it easy and enjoy the movie."

They laughed in the right places and she even sniffled once or twice—must be the wine. When the story slowed down, she found her heavy eyelids drooping over her eyes. Her head dipped to the side and hit Cole's shoulder. She jerked it upright.

"Are you falling asleep?"

"No." She put the wineglass on the table beside the sofa—right next to the bag of money. She focused on the movie again and the foolish woman who couldn't see that the hometown boy from her childhood loved her so much more than the rich fiancé from New York.

Did she have a man in her life somewhere who loved her like that? Impossible. A man like that would've moved heaven and earth to find her. A man like that would've never allowed Johnny Diamond to take her.

A man like that would be there for her, regardless of what she did or who she was.

Cole's arm crept around her shoulders and he wrapped a lock of her hair around his finger. "That fiancé guy's an idiot. He needs an ass-kicking."

She giggled, and the act must've been too much effort because she yawned at the end of it. Her head dropped to Cole's shoulder again and it felt too heavy to lift this time, so she left it there.

His arm around her tightened, and his chin rested on top of her head.

The swell of the violins indicated that the girl with the big-city job must've finally realized that the hometown boy was the one for her.

Caroline must've drifted off, because the next thing she knew, Cole had swept her up in his arms and was carrying her to the bedroom. As he placed her on the bed, she grasped his shirt, terrified of being alone, terrified of finding out who she was tomorrow.

"Don't leave me, Cole. I couldn't stand it if you left me."

The mattress dipped as he stretched out beside her on the bed, cradling her head against his chest.

"I'm not going to leave you, Caroline Johnson, or whoever the hell you are. I know you didn't kill anyone. As crazy as your story sounds, I believe it. I believe you. And whatever you did to get mixed up with Diamond, I'm going to be right by your side to see you through it."

"What if I've done something terrible? How will you be able to stand beside me?"

"If you did do something terrible, you're going to

need a friend even more. Can you trust me? If not, then this between us, right now, means nothing. But if you can, then God, I want you."

Chapter Fourteen

Oh, God. She wanted him, too. She couldn't possibly have another man waiting for her somewhere when she felt so strongly about this one. Wouldn't a husband or boyfriend be the first thing she would've remembered from her session with Dr. Shipman?

She rolled onto her side to face Cole. "I do trust you."

He brushed his warm lips across hers, while curling an arm around her waist to draw her closer. His green eyes held a question, and she wanted to answer that question with a resounding yes.

Opening her mouth against his, she slipped her hands beneath his shirt and smoothed them across the hard, flat planes of his back.

He deepened their kiss, his tongue probing her mouth before tangling with her own tongue. His hands wandered over her body, stroking, brushing, but never grabbing, as if giving her every opportunity to halt his exploration.

She didn't. She wouldn't.

She ran her fingernails along his back and trailed

them onto his belly, outlining the six-pack she'd known would be there.

He tightened his abs even more and sucked in a breath. "That tickles."

"Mmm, that's useful information." She pinched his side before grabbing the hem of his shirt. "May I?"

He raised his arms and she pulled the long-sleeved knit shirt over his head and dropped it to the floor. She skimmed her hands across his chest and along his chiseled pecs. "You're a work of art, Cole Pierson."

"And you're a tease. Why do I have my shirt off and you still have yours on?" He yanked off the sweatshirt she'd been wearing and the T-shirt beneath.

He wasted no time flicking the bra straps from her shoulders and cupping her breasts with both hands. Ducking his head, he sucked one nipple into his mouth. The pleasure of it ached between her legs, and she threw her head back in ecstasy.

As his tongue toyed with her other nipple, his hand slid to the waistband of her pants. With sure fingers, he undid her fly and peeled her jeans away from her hips.

He gave her jeans a tug. "Do you wanna help out here, or are you going to make me work for it?"

Arching her back, she lifted her hips from the mattress and he pulled down her jeans and kicked them off the foot of the bed.

His gaze hungrily devoured her body, and she tingled in all the right places. She hoped that if and when she regained her memory, she wouldn't lose Caroline's, because this was a moment she never wanted to forget.

As if in a hurry to see the rest of her, Cole unclasped

her bra and rolled her panties over her hips and down her thighs. He rolled back to his side, propping his head up with his hand, his elbow digging into the pillow.

He didn't touch her, but the way his eyes flicked over her naked body made her breasts feel heavy with desire and her pulse throb with need. She squirmed beneath his gaze, pinning her thighs together, suddenly shy.

Then, with one finger, he traced the line of her jaw and circled her throbbing lips. He pressed the pad of his thumb against her bottom lip, then dragged his finger over her chin to the base of her throat, where her pulse was fluttering wildly.

She released a small moan as his gentle, slow touch ignited a fire in her belly. When his finger skimmed over her mound and nudged between her thighs to feel her wetness, the moan turned into a gasp and she grabbed his wrist.

"Do you want me to stop?"

His voice, rough around the edges, gave her a thrill, since it revealed she wasn't the only one being tortured by unspent passion.

She hooked her fingers in the belt loops of his jeans and pulled herself closer to him. "If you stop now, I'm going to be a quivering mess, but why am I the only one who's naked here?"

"I just wanted a minute or two to…commit your body to my memory."

She blinked and gave him a shaky smile. She knew what he meant, but didn't want to acknowledge it. If there was ever a time for forgetting, it was now. She wanted only to lose herself in this moment.

"Well, now it's my turn." She unbuttoned his fly and pressed her palm against the bulge that was barely contained by his briefs. "D-do I turn you on that much?"

"You have no idea." He swung his legs over the side of the bed and pulled off his jeans, underwear and socks all at once. He reached into a pocket of his pants and pulled out his wallet. He withdrew something from the billfold and held up a condom between two fingers.

She had no idea if he'd bought that here or if he always carried a spare, but it didn't matter. It was a nod to the truth that they hardly knew each other. In fact, knew each other less than if this were a one-night stand from a bar pickup.

It didn't matter. She knew all she needed to know about Cole Pierson, and she had to have this night with him before she went to the police station tomorrow, because she may never have this chance again.

Batting her eyelashes, she whispered in a husky voice, "I like a man who's prepared."

He got back on the bed, and she nudged him onto his back. "Didn't I tell you I wanted my turn?"

She pressed the front of her body against his side, hooked her leg over his thigh and trailed her fingernails along the tight skin of his erection. She leaned over and took his brown nipple gently between her teeth as she slid her hand up and down his shaft.

Cole shivered and closed his eyes. "That feels out of this world."

She sculpted his body with her hands, kneading and stroking his warm flesh. Her lips and tongue soon followed, but she couldn't concentrate as he began to touch her—everywhere.

With a groan, he pulled her into his arms, on top of him, and scattered kisses across her face. His lips locked on to hers as he buried his hands in her hair, driving his erection between her moist thighs.

He smoothed one hand over her derriere, and their hips rocked together. Then he flipped her on her back and straddled her body, with a knee on either side of her hips. He ripped open the condom, and she took it from him.

She plucked it out of its foil packet and ran her tongue along his tip before fitting the condom over it and rolling it down the length of him.

Scooping his hands beneath her bottom, he tilted up her hips and eased into her inch by delicious inch. Once he'd entered her fully, he drew out again and drove home.

She winced and grabbed on to his shoulders. Clearly, she was no virgin, but maybe it had been a while since she'd had a man. Making love with Cole wasn't bringing back any memories—only making them.

He pulled out and nuzzled her neck. "Are you okay?"

She grasped his buttocks, digging her nails into his muscled flesh. "I will be as soon as you're back inside me."

The man didn't need an engraved invitation. He took up where he'd left off without missing a beat. As he drove into her over and over, he showered her with kisses and nipped at her breasts. He tickled her with his tongue and explored her with his fingers.

She didn't know what direction was up, and as he took her to the edge, all she could do was hold on to him.

Because she'd been riding high, his assault on her body and senses complete and unwavering, her orgasm hit her like a sledgehammer. It took her breath away and she felt like she was in a freefall from an awesome height.

When the first wave of pleasure subsided, another clawed through her belly. But before she even had time to process it, Cole's body stiffened and a sheen of sweat broke out across his smooth chest.

He raised his head and looked at her through heavy-lidded eyes. His body shook as he spent himself, and at the end, he kissed her again, like he meant it, like she would be his forever…even though she was his for this moment and this moment only.

Later, she curled up against his body, his heartbeat strong and sure beneath her cheek, his breathing deep and heavy.

Her eyelids flew open. This was the chance she'd been waiting for. With Cole sound asleep, she could slip out of this bed, grab the bag of cash and never have to show up at the police station tomorrow.

Her leg jerked and Cole murmured in his sleep. She leaned in close and peered at his strong face in the darkness.

Leave Cole? Betray him?

She snuggled in close to his body and draped her arm around his waist. Even if it turned out she was a drug trafficker and was facing twenty-five years in prison, she could never abandon Cole.

He'd given her this one night…and that's all she had to hold on to.

COLE BLINKED AGAINST the morning light leaking through the blinds. He bolted upright, a shot of adrenaline spiking through his system. He flung his arm to the side and swept it across the cool…empty sheet.

He rolled off the bed, scrambling for his jeans. Barefoot and buttoning his fly, he crashed into the living room and made a beeline for the bag of cash next to the sofa. He plunged his hand into the canvas bag and pulled out the stacks of money. Was it all there?

"Caroline?" He cranked his head around the small room, which gave him a view of the empty kitchen. He'd passed the bathroom on the way to the living room, and she wasn't in there, either.

How could he have allowed himself to be duped that way? It had been what she'd wanted all along—the food, the offers of booze, the sex.

She'd wanted an escape—and he'd handed it to her because he couldn't keep it in his pants.

As he shoveled the money back into the bag, the front door swung open and Caroline stepped across the threshold with a paper bag clutched against her chest with one arm.

She froze, her gaze tracking from the money bag to his face. "What are you doing?"

"Just checking on the money."

She kicked the door closed behind her. "Just checking on me, you mean. You thought I skipped out."

"I did have a second of panic. I'm sorry."

She walked past him, swinging the bag. "I could act aggrieved and insulted, but I'm all about the truth today and the truth is, I woke up in the middle of the night and the thought crossed my mind."

"What stopped you?"

"You." She plopped the bag on the kitchen counter. "So, I don't blame you for thinking the worst when you woke up alone this morning."

"I still feel guilty." He joined her in the kitchen, where she was pulling eggs, milk and bacon out of the bag.

"That makes two of us." She held up the package of bacon. "But I'm going to atone for my guilt by cooking you breakfast—all ingredients courtesy of Linda."

"And I'll atone for mine by helping you, but I don't want to cook shirtless." He returned to the bedroom to put on his shirt from last night, visited the bathroom briefly, then sidled up next to her at the counter. "Put me to work."

She handed him a pan for the bacon and started cracking eggs in a bowl. "Is the Port Angeles Police Department going to call me today or do they expect me to call them? Or is it the sheriff's department that's going to call?"

"It's the Port Angeles Police. They'll call you with a time to come in. They've probably dusted the office for prints and will want to compare yours to any they found. And will share whatever they have with the homicide detectives." Cole peeled off several slices of bacon and lined them up in the skillet.

"That may be a surprise for all of us."

"I'll protect you, Caroline. If something turns up on your prints, I can tell them you're with us, with the DEA."

"And then you'll take me in yourself?" She beat the eggs with a fork, the tines clinking against the glass bowl in a furious rhythm.

"If you're involved with Johnny Diamond in any way, we'll have to deal with it. You know that, right? I can't just let you walk away."

"I know that you have to do your job, Cole." She gave him a watery smile. "Can we just enjoy breakfast until that time comes?"

He came up behind her and wrapped his arms around her waist. "Absolutely. And while you're waiting for the call, I'm going to check out the mysterious stranger from the shop and Sutter's—the one supposedly buying real estate. Do you have any idea where he's staying?"

"None, but maybe we can tail Rebecca Geist, the Realtor. She's the only one I know for sure who's been in contact with him." Caroline waved a fork at the TV. "Do you think the local news will have anything new on Dr. Shipman?"

"We? Did you just say we can tail her?"

"I sort of figured you wouldn't want to leave my side, because I just admitted I had thoughts of fleeing last night."

He kissed her neck. "That's not the only reason I don't want to leave your side."

Turning to face him, she curled her arms around his waist. "Whatever happens, I'm glad it was you in Timberline looking for me."

A sizzle and pop from the frying bacon interrupted the kiss he was about to plant on her mouth. He pulled away from her and prodded the bacon with a fork. "When we finish breakfast, let's go back to my hotel so I can shower and change. Is Linda opening the shop today?"

"She is, but I already talked to her this morning when I picked up the food and told her that I'd be waiting for a call from the police, so she told me to take the day off." Caroline poured the egg mixture in the pan next to his. "Of course, once I get arrested, I'll be taking a lot of days off."

"It won't go down like that, Caroline." *At least not at first.*

She bumped her hip against his. "However it goes down, I'm ready to face it."

She might be ready to face it, but was he?

An hour later, after they'd finished breakfast and Caroline had showered and changed into a pair of black jeans and a blue sweater that matched her eyes, they drove into the parking lot of his hotel, a newer one located away from the town center and closer to Evergreen Software.

He wanted to stop by the hotel gift shop, buy more condoms and bed her again in his hotel room, but she had a nervous, faraway look in her eyes after listening to a news report on the radio about Dr. Shipman's murder.

The trauma of what she'd experienced yesterday

seemed to hit her out of the blue, and she'd stop talking and start twisting her fingers into knots. Cole had dealt with enough crime scenes and enough people not accustomed to the gore to recognize the symptoms.

He gave the gift shop a sideways glance as they passed it on their way to the bank of elevators. He punched the call button with more force than necessary and Caroline gave him a sharp glance.

When they got up to the room, he turned on the TV, but selected a movie channel. She didn't need to watch any more news. "You can help yourself to the mini bar while I'm in the shower."

"Do I look like I need a drink at ten o'clock in the morning?"

"There's other stuff in there."

"I don't need any distractions, Cole. I'm not going to watch the news, if that's what you're worried about."

"Just try to relax."

To his disappointment, she didn't come in to check on him once during his shower, so he wrapped a towel around his waist and checked on her instead.

She was sitting on the edge of the bed, watching a crime show, her jaw set and her hands clutching the folds of the bedspread.

He sat next to her and took one of her hands in his. "It's going to be okay."

"It's my fault Dr. Shipman was murdered. If I had never gone to see her, the people after me never would've targeted her." Caroline looked at him, her blue eyes filling with tears. "And you know the worst part?

I lied to her. I never even gave her a chance to refuse me as a patient because of the danger."

"Do you think she would've refused to see you? I don't. She probably suspected more than you were telling her. Don't blame yourself, Caroline."

"Stop calling me Caroline." She jumped up from the bed. "It's not even my name. Do you know where I got that name? The trucker who picked me up down the road from the Stardust had Carolina plates. That's how real I am."

Cole rose from the bed and wrapped his arms around her trembling body. "You're real to me. Whatever's in your past is just that—past. And if it happens to be something bad, you're not that person anymore. Knowing you like I do now, I can't believe you've done anything criminal in your past, and I know criminals."

A tear ran down her face and she buried her head against his chest. "I don't want to disappoint you. I don't want to see that look fade from your eyes when you look at me and realize…"

"Not going to happen." He pulled away before his desire for her became too obvious. "I'm going to put some clothes on, and then let's have a look around Timberline together. Now that I know everything, maybe I can help you remember why you're here, why you had that scrap of paper in your pocket."

"Are you going to hypnotize me?" Her gaze dropped to the towel slipping down his hips.

He grabbed the towel before it slipped any farther. "I would if I could, but I don't know jack about hypnosis. You went through a session already. Do you think you could practice some self-hypnosis?"

"I could give it a try."

"I know you've been afraid to remember, but maybe now that you're open to the truth, you can force your memories to come back."

"Maybe you're right, but now—" she pressed her hand against her forehead "—nothing is there."

"You've had a lot to deal with. Stop stressing over things you can't change." He picked up the remote and aimed it at the TV. "And stop watching these crime shows. Find a comedy."

He tossed the remote on the bed and headed back to the bathroom after sweeping up some clothes. Several minutes later, when he entered the other room fully dressed, the TV was silent and Caroline was reclining on the bed against a stack of pillows with her eyes closed.

He crept toward his boots in the corner of the room, and she opened one eye. "I'm trying."

"Good. Now let's go take Timberline by storm and see if you can remember anything."

As they walked down the hallway toward the elevator, Caroline peered over the railing down to the lobby. She choked and grabbed his arm. "Cole, that man. He must've followed us. He's down there, in the foyer."

"What?" Cole crowded next to her and looked down four floors to the spacious area. "Where?"

"He just crossed in front of the reception desk. He might be going out that side door to the parking lot."

Cole took off for the stairwell and banged through the fire door, with Caroline trailing behind him. He wanted to tell her to stay back, but he didn't know what the man looked like.

Cole ran down four flights of stairs, and she kept up with him all the way. When he reached the bottom, he burst through the final door into the lobby. "Which way?"

Panting, she pointed to the right of the check-in desk.

As he headed for the side door leading to a parking lot, she grabbed on to his belt loop to keep up. "What are you going to do?"

"I'm going to find out who the hell he is." Cole pushed through the glass door. "Do you see him?"

Caroline tugged on his sleeve. "Over there, at the trunk of that white car."

With clenched fists and a heart beating out of his chest, Cole strode toward the man as he closed the trunk. "Hey! You!"

The man turned with a scowl on his face, and then he saw Caroline and his eyes bugged out of their sockets. He reached into the pocket of his raincoat, and Cole charged him, knocking him against the car and pinning his arms under his body.

"What the hell is wrong with you?" The man bucked and loosened one of his arms. He took a swing and Cole blocked the punch.

"I'm a DEA agent. I'd think twice before assaulting me."

The man slumped. "What do you want? I haven't

done anything wrong. You can check my trunk. Do you think I have drugs or something?"

Cole plunged his hand in the man's coat pocket and pulled out a glove. "Do you have any weapons on you?"

"Weapons? No. I told you, I haven't done anything wrong. I'm just getting into my rental car, for goodness sake."

Cole released him and fished for his badge. He flipped it open so the man could get a good look at it. "Open your trunk for me."

The man seemed unsure of Cole's authority, but complied, anyway.

The lid popped and Cole lifted it, his gaze scanning the cargo space, empty except for a gift basket filled with sweets.

He backed up and slammed it shut. "What's your name and why are you bothering Ms. Johnson?"

Caroline made a sudden movement beside him and sucked in a breath.

"I'm sorry." The man tugged at the lapels of his trench coat as he turned toward Caroline. "I didn't know I was bothering you. You're the woman from the tourist shop, right?"

"Yes. He's… I'm… We're just overreacting."

Cole raised his eyebrows. She'd been worrying about this guy for a few days and *now* they were overreacting. "Wait a minute. You felt threatened by him. Let's at least see who he is."

"You felt I was threatening you?" The man slicked a hand over his shaved head. "I'm so sorry. I never meant to make you feel that way."

"Who are you? Can we start there? As you saw, I'm Cole Pierson with the DEA, and this is Caroline Johnson."

"I'm James Brice, and I'm going to reach for my wallet in my back pocket." He did so and showed Cole his New York driver's license. "I'm in town for business. I bought a stuffed frog from Caroline a few days ago. I had no idea I had made her uneasy."

"I'm sorry." Caroline crossed her hands over her chest. "I have some other things going on in my life right now, and I think I just projected onto you."

Brice held up his palms. "No harm done."

Cole stuck out his hand. "Sorry, man. We've both been on edge."

Brice shook his hand and opened the car door.

As Cole took a few steps back to the hotel, his hand on Caroline's back, he furrowed his brow. *Brice.*

He stopped and pivoted. "Are you any relation to Heather Brice, one of the children kidnapped as part of the Timberline Trio?"

Brice didn't turn from his car, but his shoulders slumped. "Heather was my little sister. I'm in town to sell my parents' property here, but was trying to keep a low profile."

Caroline covered her mouth. "I am so sorry."

Brice faced them, his back against the car. "In fact, that's why I may have shown a little more interest in you than appeared normal, Caroline."

She tilted her head. "Why?"

"Because when I first saw you in that shop—I thought you were my kidnapped sister."

Chapter Fifteen

All the blood drained from her head and she felt like she was going to pitch forward, face-first.

Cole must've sensed her shock, or maybe she'd already started her free fall, because he put an arm around her shoulders.

"Me?" Her voice squeaked and she cleared her throat. "Why would you think that?"

"Just something about the look of you. I learned later that you were new to town and related to Linda Gunderson, the owner of Timberline Treasures." James shrugged. "It happens now and then. I'll see a woman about the age my sister would have been, and do a double take. Wishful thinking, I guess."

Cole asked, "Does anyone in Timberline know you're here?"

"Only Rebecca Geist. She's helping me list the properties. They're mostly commercial or vacant lots. After the kidnapping, my parents didn't have the heart to stay here."

"Did the FBI notify your parents that they ID'd Rocky Whitecotton for the crimes?"

"They did. That's why I'm here. Maybe they felt a sense of closure after that news."

At the mention of Rocky's name, Caroline almost doubled over as her stomach churned. Somehow this was all connected, and she might even be connected to the kidnapping of this man's sister. Maybe she even had information about the kidnappings buried in her brain.

Cole asked, "Did your parents ever suspect Rocky?"

"Not that I know of, but they don't speak of it— ever." James spread his hands. "Look, I'm sorry for the misunderstanding, but I'm asking you to keep this to yourselves. I want to fly under the radar while I'm here taking care of my family's business."

"No problem."

As they turned away, Caroline twisted her head over her shoulder and said, "Sorry. Sorry…for your loss."

James nodded and slammed the car door, peeling out of the parking lot seconds later.

Caroline chewed on her bottom lip as they returned to the hotel.

Cole opened the door for her. "I feel stupid. Poor guy."

"Yeah, that's my fault. I'm sorry for dragging you into it, but at least I wasn't totally imagining things. He *was* interested in me—just not how I thought he was."

"At least I don't have to track him down now."

"What if I know something about his sister? About all the kidnapped kids?"

"I thought about that, but the kidnappings occurred twenty-five years ago. I doubt Rocky Whitecotton is still talking about his past crimes. If he's connected to

Johnny Diamond, I'm sure he has new crimes to talk about." Cole snapped his fingers. "That reminds me. I contacted my partner about looking into any connections Diamond could've had with Whitecotton."

"I thought Rocky Whitecotton had fallen off the face of the earth?"

"That's my understanding, but he's not someone we ever had on our radar—at least not recently. The FBI may have moved him back up their list based on the new information regarding the kidnappings, but we've never searched for him."

"Are we still going to explore Timberline to see if anything jogs my memory?"

"Yeah, give me a minute in the room to call my partner, Craig."

As Cole talked to his partner, Caroline called Linda to check up on her.

"Have you gone to the sheriff's station yet?"

Caroline corrected her. "Police station. Not yet. I'm still leaving Timberline, Linda, even though I'm so grateful for everything you did."

"I know you are." The bells on the shop door jingled. "Customer just walked in. We'll talk later."

Caroline ended the call with a tear trembling on her eyelash. She might not have another opportunity to talk to Linda again.

A few minutes later, Cole ended his own call. "That's interesting. Still no leads on Whitecotton. Unless he changed his name and went into some kind of criminals' witness protection program, he really has disappeared. Maybe he was smuggled out of the country."

Caroline dropped her phone. "Spanish."

"What?"

"I told you I knew Spanish."

"You told me you could understand some Spanish on a TV show."

"It's more than that, Cole. I can speak Spanish fluently." She tried it out, the words and phrases coming to her lips naturally.

Cole spoke Spanish, too, and kept up the conversation for another minute. He switched back to English. "As far as I can tell, you have a dialect from Mexico."

"Really? You can hear that?"

"I'm not great at it. My partner's better." He held out his phone. "Would you be willing to talk to him? His name's Craig Delgado."

"Of course."

He placed a call to his partner again and gave him some background on her that left out all the bad parts. Then he put the phone on speaker and handed it to her.

She and Craig spoke for a few minutes—about the weather, about the Timberline landscape and about Cole—until he snatched the phone from her.

"What do you think, Craig?"

"I think I'd better continue giving her the lowdown on you."

Cole rolled his eyes at Caroline. "I mean about the accent."

"Yeah, that's definitely Mexico. I'd go even further and say northern interior, maybe around Chihuahua."

Caroline leaned toward the phone in Cole's hand. "Is that a desert climate, Craig?"

"It can be. The Chihuahua Desert extends from New Mexico all the way down south into Mexico."

"Craig, does the FBI have any leads on Whitecotton going to Mexico?"

"I can check on it, and you know our boy Johnny Diamond made several trips down there—illegal ones."

"Check out Whitecotton for me."

"When are you coming back from your so-called vacation?"

"Dude, I think that vacation just ended."

His conversation with Craig over, Cole tapped the phone against his chin. "You may have been down in Mexico with these guys."

Caroline folded her arms over the knots forming in her belly. "I'm scared, Cole. What was I doing with them? What was I doing in Mexico?"

"Your fingerprints might tell us everything we need to know."

She uncrossed her arms and studied the tips of her fingers as if she could read her past there. She saw nothing.

Cole took both her hands and pressed her palms against his chest. "It's going to be okay, Car..."

He stopped when she flashed him a look. She wasn't going to lash out at him for calling her Caroline again. He was just trying to help, but he was dreaming. He wanted to rescue her because he hadn't been able to rescue his wife from her demons.

"It's not going to be all right, is it? I know you're trying to make me feel better, but my situation keeps getting worse and worse."

"You know what might make you feel better?" He pressed a kiss against the inside of her left wrist. "Let's get out of this hotel room and explore Timberline. It's better than waiting around for the police to call."

"You're right." She flipped her hair over her shoulder. "I'm going to face everything head-on today."

As Caroline buckled her seat belt in his car, she said, "Where to first?"

"How about Evergreen Software? Have you been there yet?"

"You think I came here for Evergreen Software?"

"Let's take a drive to the facility. You never know. We're close by, anyway."

About five minutes later, Caroline took in the modern white buildings that comprised the Evergreen campus, but she felt no twinges of recognition or familiarity. "I don't think I came back for this, Cole."

"It's impressive though, isn't it? I thought I read somewhere that the Brice family had some property out here, too, that they sold to Evergreen."

"I felt sorry for James Brice."

"Yeah, I slammed him against that car pretty hard."

Caroline punched Cole's arm. "Not that. He seemed sad to be here wrapping up everything for his parents."

"I don't blame the parents for taking off. I can't imagine what they went through—to lose a child like that."

"And the guilt."

"Guilt?" He swung through the Evergreen parking lot once more before exiting the facility. "Why would they feel guilty?"

"I think there would always be that element of what

you could've done differently as a parent. Just those three were taken. Why those three? Did the bikers who were involved in the kidnappings ever say why?"

"Those bikers were all dead by the time the truth came out. Only Dax Kennedy is still around, and he was a younger member of the motorcycle gang at the time and wasn't directly involved in the kidnapping."

"Well, I'm sure those parents drove themselves crazy wondering why. The siblings, too. Poor James."

"It was hard on the siblings. In fact, the kidnapped boy's brother duplicated the kidnappings just a few months ago."

"Oh, my God. This town has been through a lot. Was Johnny Diamond involved in the kidnappings? Maybe that's how he knows Rocky."

"He wasn't around then, too young, but there's no doubt that his membership in the Lords of Chaos connects him to Whitecotton." Cole pulled up to a fork in the road and idled the engine. "Do you want to head to the forest? There are a couple of nice trails out there. The peace and tranquility might do you good."

She checked the time on her phone. "Especially since the police department should be calling anytime now. They did say afternoon, right?"

"They might be waiting for all the fingerprints to come in, but I'm guessing there were a lot in Dr. Shipman's office."

"Speaking of guilt." Caroline squeezed her eyes shut. "She would be off on her trip right now if I hadn't become her patient."

"I know it's hard, Caroline, but you need to put the blame on her killer."

She sat forward suddenly. "Can we stop by Linda's shop on our way through town? I want to check up on her."

"Did she sound okay on the phone?"

"She did, but she had a rough time of it the other night and maybe she's trying to get back on her feet too quickly."

"Especially if it was poison." Cole jerked the steering wheel to the right to go into downtown Timberline. "She's a fighter, that one."

As Cole's car traveled down Main Street, Caroline spotted flashing emergency lights ahead, and butterflies swirled in her stomach. "Look at that."

"Excitement in downtown Timberline. I hope nobody's hurt."

"Cole." She grabbed his thigh, digging her fingernails into the denim of his jeans. "Is that ambulance in front of Timberline Treasures?"

He swore. "It looks like it is."

"Hurry, hurry." She sat up, straining against the seat belt, her heart thundering in her chest.

"I can't get any closer. I'm pulling up here."

When he parked the car, Caroline tumbled from the passenger side and ran down the sidewalk. She pushed through the clutch of people gathered near the door of Linda's shop. "Let me by."

Quentin Stevens, one of the Timberline Sheriff's Department deputies, held up his hand as she charged toward the door. "Hold on, please."

"Is it Linda Gunderson? I'm her…cousin."

Deputy Stevens's eyes widened. "Are you Caroline?"

"Yes, yes."

Cole had caught up with her and placed a steadying hand on her back. "What happened, Deputy?"

"Aggravated assault and robbery."

Caroline covered her mouth. "Assault? Someone assaulted Linda?"

"I'm afraid so."

"Is—is she…alive?"

"She's alive, sustained some injuries."

"I need to see her."

"She's been asking for you, so go on in, but she's being treated so don't get in the way of the EMTs doing their job."

Caroline grabbed Cole's hand, dragging him along with her in case Stevens tried to stop him.

She bolted toward Linda, who was bloodied and stretched out on a gurney, with two EMTs cleaning her wounds and taking her vitals.

Caroline cried out and dropped to the side of the gurney, clutching Linda's hand. "Oh, my God. What happened?"

Linda parted swollen lips, but no sound came out.

Another deputy tapped Caroline on the shoulder. "You're Ms. Gunderson's cousin?"

She rose to face him. "Yes, can you tell me what happened? Is Linda going to be okay?"

"You'll have to ask the EMTs about that." He shook Cole's hand. "I'm Deputy Unger."

"Cole Pierson. This is Caroline Johnson. Do you know what went down in here?"

"Ms. Gunderson's having a hard time communicating, but it sounds like a man entered the shop, threatened her with a knife and took all the money from the register. Why he felt he had to beat her up is a mystery to me. Must be some kind of sadist or hard-core criminal."

Caroline leaned against Cole for support. "It—it was a robbery? He stole her money?"

"Yeah, in broad daylight, too." The officer shook his head. "Sometimes I wonder what Evergreen Software is bringing in, with all the jobs and revitalization."

One of the EMTs spoke up. "Ma'am, we're taking her to emergency if you want to come by the hospital later."

"Was she injured badly?"

"She has a nasty cut on her head and she lost a lot of blood. I'm surprised she's still conscious, but she's hanging in there."

Caroline felt a soft tap against her calf and crouched beside the gurney.

Linda grabbed on to Caroline's sleeve and pulled.

Caroline moved closer as Linda mouthed some words.

"What is it?"

Linda shifted her eyes to the deputy and then whispered in Caroline's ear. "The man wanted information about you. I told him the story you made up."

Chapter Sixteen

Linda's head fell to the side as her eyes closed and her mouth gaped open.

Caroline choked. "What's wrong? What's wrong with her?"

"She lost consciousness. We're moving her now. Back up, please."

As Cole helped Caroline to her feet, the EMTs expanded the legs of the gurney and wheeled Linda out of the store to the waiting ambulance.

The deputies asked Caroline a few more questions, and while they continued collecting evidence from the store and dusting for prints, she sat in the corner with her hands pinned between her knees, Linda's whisper echoing in her head.

Someone had roughed up her friend trying to get information about *her*, and it seemed that Linda had known she'd been lying all along.

When Deputy Stevens stopped by to tell her they'd wrapped things up for now, she said, "Did Linda give a description of the man? Did anyone on the street see him leaving the store?"

"White guy, but dark complexion, wore his hair in a ponytail."

Caroline furrowed her brow. "D-did she tell you what he said to her?"

"Told her to hand over the money in the register and to be quick about it. After he stuffed the money in his pockets, he came around the counter and hit her. Knocked her to the ground and kicked her."

Caroline gasped and nausea claimed her stomach. "Anything else? Did he say anything else?"

"Nope. Headed out the back door to the alley." Stevens waved his hand in the air. "You can stay here if you'd like to clean up. We have what we need and it's no longer a crime scene, but you may want to close up shop for the day."

So, Linda had lied for her again.

"I will, thanks."

When all the deputies had left the store and only a few people remained on the sidewalk out front, Caroline locked the door and flipped over the sign to read Closed.

She sank back in the chair while Cole paced through the racks.

"This is too much of a coincidence. This has to be connected to Johnny Diamond and…you," he finally muttered.

"It is."

"I don't know why this guy came in here and robbed Linda and then knocked her around, but he was probably hoping to find you here, and then covered his tracks."

"He didn't even cover his tracks."

Cole stopped pacing like a caged animal and stationed himself in front of her. "How do you know?"

"Linda told me."

"Linda told you what?" His green eyes narrowed to slits, making him look like a dangerous jungle cat. "She could barely speak and then passed out."

"She whispered to me, Cole. She told me the man was trying to get information about me. She told me she stuck with my story."

"Oh, God." He spanned his forehead with one hand and massaged his temples. "He must've demanded answers and then punched her when he didn't get the ones he wanted. Miserable coward."

"This has to end. Everything and everyone I touch is getting destroyed."

"Wait. So Linda knew you weren't telling the truth all this time?"

"I guess she must've suspected something was off. Maybe it was when I thought someone had searched my place."

"She turned out to be a loyal friend."

"Too loyal." Caroline's cell phone buzzed and she pulled it from her pocket. The number on the display didn't even send terror into her heart like she'd thought it would. "Hello."

"Ms. Johnson, this is Detective Rowan with Clallam County Homicide. We're ready to take your prints now at the Port Angeles Police Department. Can you come in this afternoon?"

"I'll be there."

COLE GLANCED SIDEWAYS at Caroline. She'd been so quiet since leaving Timberline Treasures, blaming herself for everything, no doubt.

She'd called the hospital before they left for Port Angeles, and the nurse on duty told her Linda had some swelling on the brain and they were keeping her in a coma for now, but that she was out of immediate danger.

At least the thug who'd beat up Linda must know by now that Caroline wouldn't or couldn't spill the beans about whatever they were afraid of. If they wanted Diamond's money back from Caroline, they were out of luck. The DEA had it now.

"We're almost there. Are you ready?" Cole squeezed her knee and it bounced under his touch.

"I am ready. What's the plan?"

"We'll walk in and get you fingerprinted. Then they'll run them to verify your identity, which can take about thirty minutes."

"They're not going to come back to a Caroline Johnson, so then what?"

"If you have a criminal record, I'll step in at that point and tell them that you're working with the DEA. Then we'll research everything there is to know about your real identity before I…bring you in."

Her lips puckered for a soft whistle. "And what happens if the prints come back for someone who *doesn't* have a criminal record—but the name isn't Caroline Johnson?"

"Again, I'll step in and make up some plausible story. Even if you weren't a criminal in your other life, technically it's illegal to give a false name to the police, but I can smooth that over for you."

She traced the knuckles of his hand, still on her knee. "You've done that a lot, Cole. Thanks."

"And once we find out you don't have a criminal past, I'm going to get you the best psychiatrist in the world and you're going to get better."

"Then I'll help you figure out the connection between Johnny Diamond, Rocky Whitecotton and the Timberline Trio."

The police station came into view. Caroline's posture stiffened and she licked her lips.

She jumped out of the car and made a beeline for the station, staring straight ahead, placing one foot in front of the other as if afraid to veer off course.

Cole took a few long strides to catch up with her and opened the door of the facility, placing a steadying hand on Caroline's back. The Port Angeles station was small, as befitted a small town. Detective Rowan from the county wasn't going to be here, but the Port Angeles cops were under orders to email the results to him immediately.

Cole might have to make his case for Caroline to Rowan instead of the small-town cops.

The officer at the front counter looked up. "Can I help you?"

Caroline shook off Cole's hand and stepped up to the window. "I'm Caroline Johnson. I found Dr. Jules Shipman's body and I'm here to get fingerprinted, since I didn't have any ID on me—and still don't."

"Oh, right. Officer Farella is expecting you." He left

the front desk and ducked into the back, with another officer trailing him.

Another man opened the door on the side. "Come on back, Ms. Johnson. I'm Officer Farella. I'll be doing the honors today." He extended his hand and Caroline shook it.

Farella reached past Caroline, hand outstretched. "You must be Agent Pierson with the DEA, right?"

"Good to meet you." Cole shook the other man's hand, sizing him up. Didn't seem like a hard-ass that would play hardball, but you never knew.

"Dr. Shipman's murder isn't something the DEA is interested in, is it?"

"Can't say right now. You understand."

"Sure, sure." Farella swept his arm to the side, indicating a cubicle with a table, scanner and computer inside. "Ms. Johnson, after you. Have a seat in front of the scanner."

Cole pulled out the chair for her and she perched on the edge of it, eyeing the machine.

"You've probably never had this done before, ma'am, but it works just like a scanner. We'll do one finger at a time and then your palms."

Caroline followed Farella's instructions, the muscles in her face strained and tight, her cheekbones protruding sharply.

When he finished, he entered a code and pressed some buttons. "This computer will send your prints automatically to the Washington State Department of Justice, which is connected to the national database. It takes about half an hour. We have some coffee here, but the stuff next door at the Coffee Grinder is a lot better, and I have Ms. Johnson's cell phone number so I can call when we have a match."

"Thanks, we'll wait next door." Cole helped Caroline, who seemed incapable of moving, to her feet and led her out of the station.

Once on the sidewalk, she collapsed against him. "I'm so nervous."

"Then you probably don't need any caffeine. Do you want some decaf tea instead or something else?"

"Tea is fine." She reached for her phone. "I'm going to call the hospital to check on Linda's condition."

While he ordered a tea for her and a coffee for himself, Caroline found a table and got on her phone. She'd ended the call before he made it to the table, a cup in each hand.

"How's she doing? Out of the coma yet?"

"Not yet, but it's just a precaution at this point due to her age. They think she's going to pull out of it just fine."

"That's a relief. We're almost at the end of the line. We're going to have answers."

"*I'm* almost at the end of the line."

He drew a circle on the inside of her wrist with the tip of his finger. "I'll do whatever I can for you."

She dredged her tea bag through the steaming water. "And I'll do whatever I can for you, to make up for everything—the secrets, the lies."

"You have amnesia. I think that excuses a lot."

"You know one thing I do remember?"

He hunched forward and she held up her finger. "About the immediate past, not my past life."

"Yeah?"

"The description that Linda gave of her attacker sort of matches the description of a man I saw in Dr. Shipman's office—the only person I saw in Dr. Shipman's office. He was coming in as I was leaving my first appointment."

"Dark-complected Caucasian with long hair?"

"Yes, only his hair wasn't in a ponytail. It was loose and kind of scraggly. He kept his head down, so I didn't get a look at his face."

"You should report that to the deputies in Timberline."

"I think I have a lot to report to a lot of deputies and detectives and DEA agents."

Cole checked his phone with a frown. "It's been thirty-five minutes."

Her blue eyes brightened. "That's encouraging. If I were on the FBI's most-wanted list, you'd think the Port Angeles police would be storming this place with guns blazing."

"Farella probably got busy and hasn't checked the computer lately." Cole stood up and held out his hand. "Are you ready to meet your fate?"

"As long as you're by my side." She put her palm in his. "Bring it on."

He kept hold of her hand as they walked back to the station. His next hold on her might be completely different. As they got to the door, he dropped it—didn't want Farella to think there was anything more between them.

They walked up to the window and Farella came from the back, a piece of paper clutched in his hand and creases lining his face.

"Ma'am, we have a problem."

Cole swore under his breath as Caroline laced her fingers in front of her.

She cleared her throat. "What's the problem, Officer Farella?"

"There are no fingerprint records for you in the state of Washington—or anywhere else in the nation. It's like you don't even exist."

Chapter Seventeen

Caroline sagged against Cole's side as relief flooded her senses. She wasn't a criminal. She wouldn't be going to jail or some psychiatric facility today.

"Th-that's odd, I guess."

"That *is* unusual." Cole rubbed his chin as if this were some great mystery.

"Would I have fingerprints on file if I never committed a crime or held some job where I needed to be fingerprinted?"

Farella spread his hands. "Never had anything notarized? Never bought property? Some states even require fingerprints on the application for driver's licenses. It's just very unusual today for someone to have no fingerprints on file. Are you sure you're not in a witness-protection program?"

His words punched her in the gut, and Caroline grabbed Cole's sleeve and sucked in a quick breath.

Farella chuckled, glancing from her face to Cole's. "I was just kidding…I think."

"What next?" Cole asked. "You'll need to report this to Detective Rowan."

"Yeah, I'll send him the results and he can check your prints against the ones we took in the office to rule them out. We may have a lead on the killer, anyway."

"Can you reveal anything?"

"Not much. A witness saw a man in the alley behind Dr. Shipman's office around the time of the murder. We're working with that person now."

"Is that it for me?" Caroline shoved her nervous hands in her pockets.

"That's it for now—at least we know you're not some criminal on the run." Farella chuckled again and Caroline laughed along with him with giddy abandon.

She held up her cell phone. "Well, you and Detective Rowan have my number if you need anything else."

"We probably will. When we catch this guy we'll have a trial, if he doesn't plead out, and you'll most likely be called as a witness." Farella shook his finger in her face. "Let's just hope you have your ID by then."

"God, I hope so."

She and Cole left the station silently and she kept her lips sealed until they got to his rental car. Once she closed the door, she let out a scream that bounced off the windows.

Cole covered his ears. "You really are a mystery woman."

"But I'm not a criminal, right?" She grabbed his arm, her fingers sinking into the slick material of his jacket. "If I were, my fingerprints would've been in the system."

Chewing on his bottom lip, Cole adjusted the rear-view mirror, checking for tails like he always did. "I don't want to rain on your parade, but it just means you were never *arrested* for a crime. It doesn't mean you never committed one."

She slumped in her seat. "You still believe I was involved in some criminal activity with Johnny Diamond?"

"No, just doing a reality check."

"Well, in my reality, as slim as that is, I'm clear. Now I just have to discover who I am and what I was doing with Diamond." She took his hand. "Can you help me? I'm officially turning myself in to the DEA. I'll make a statement and everything. I'll repeat for the record all I know about my time with Johnny at the Stardust Motel, and you can get someone to pick my brain apart, hypnotize me or whatever it takes to bring back my memories."

He brought her hand to his lips and kissed it. "Sounds like a plan."

"I want to visit Linda in the hospital. Can you take me there? When she's better, I'm going to tell her everything. Once I'm officially in your custody, Diamond's associates will figure any drug money I took is in the hands of the DEA. They won't be able to get to me and it'll be worthless for them to hurt anyone else close to me."

"I'll take you to the hospital, but I'll wait there with you."

"Do you still think I'm going to make a run for it? I'd just be putting myself in further danger if I did."

"I'm not worried about that, but until you're safely in our custody, Diamond's cohorts will be out to get you."

They drove back to Timberline and Caroline peppered him with questions about the fingerprints. "Is it really that unusual for someone not to have prints in the national database?"

"These days, it is. For adults, anyway." He drummed his thumbs on the steering wheel. "Caroline, do you think it's possible that you lived in Mexico? The Chihuahua Desert, the Spanish speaking?"

A spike of fear pounded her poor, addled brain. "If I had been living in Mexico, would that explain why I have no fingerprints on file in the US?"

"It could."

She turned to stare out at the green, watery landscape flying by.

It seemed that all roads led to Mexico.

Linda's doctors had moved her to a room in the hospital next to the emergency facility. Cole drove to the main hospital and left the car in the parking structure.

As they stood in front of the elevator, he said, "I'm going to walk you up to Linda's floor, and then I'm going to make a few calls. I'll notify the DEA office in San Diego about you. They'll want you to come in right away."

"As soon as I get Linda's friends on board to take care of her while I'm gone. But how am I going to get on an airplane without a driver's license?"

"The DEA will handle everything."

They rode the elevator up to Linda's floor and Caroline approached the nurses' station. "I'm Caroline

Johnson. I'm here to see Linda Gunderson. The doctors okayed it over the phone."

The nurse clicked her keyboard, and Caroline looked over her shoulder at Cole, who was against the wall by the stairwell, on his phone.

"You can go right ahead, Ms. Johnson. She's in room 528. She's sharing, so please don't disturb the other occupant."

"Thanks." Caroline waved to Cole to get his attention, and then pointed down the hallway. He nodded.

Her low-heeled boots clicked on the linoleum as she passed every room, checking the number. She found Linda's room at the end of the hall and pushed open the door.

Her heart skipped a beat when she saw the monitors and tubes hooked up to her friend. She eased into the plastic chair next to the bed and took Linda's hand. "Hang in there, Linda. I'm going to tell you everything when you come out of this."

The patient on the other side of the curtain coughed.

As Caroline held Linda's hand, the cell phone in her pocket buzzed. She hoped the police hadn't suddenly discovered something about her fingerprints.

She pulled the phone out and screwed up her mouth as she glanced at Linda's number coming through. How was Linda calling from her phone when she was lying in a coma in this bed? Maybe one of her friends had gotten hold of Linda's cell.

"Hello?"

"You listen and you listen good. Your little game is over…*Caroline*. You're coming back with us right now and you're handing over all of Johnny's money— *our* money."

The harsh voice grated against her ear and the phone almost slipped from her grip.

"I don't know who you are. I don't know who any of you are. I lost my memory when Johnny threw me across the room. Don't you get it?"

"But you remember that Johnny threw you across the room?"

"That and that he tried to kill me."

"He wasn't trying to kill you, just bring you back. That's all we want. Nobody's going to hurt you. Don't you want to be with your family again?"

A sob rose in her throat. She wanted a family more than anything. She wanted an identity more than anything—just not her real one. "It's too late. I'm turning myself in to the DEA."

The man swore. "Is that who that cop is? He's DEA?"

"Yes, and he knows everything that I know, and I'm going to get my memory back and he's going to know even more. H-he's standing right here listening to everything I say."

The man laughed, which ended in a cough. "You're in a hospital room alone with a comatose patient right now."

Caroline jumped from the chair and glanced over her shoulder. "You're watching me?"

"How's your friend, the shop owner?"

A chill dripped down her spine. "She's hurt, thanks to you."

"She's gonna be hurting a lot more if you don't do

what I tell you to do. Got it? That one, the DEA agent once we figure out who he is—and we will—and your sister. You remember your sister, don't you? Or maybe you don't. She's still in Mexico with her family, but we can get to all of them if you don't come with me now."

A sister? She had a sister? Her head began to throb and she massaged the base of her skull. "What do you want?"

"Told you. We want you to come home. Once you regain your memory, you'll want to come home, too."

"Apparently not. Why was I on the run in the first place? Because that's why I was with Johnny, wasn't it. You or Rocky sent him."

Silence stretched on the other end of the line and then the man said, "So you remember Rocky?"

"N-no. I just saw his text to Johnny, after Johnny was dead."

"Does that DEA agent know about Rocky?"

"No."

"I thought you told him everything?"

"Not everything, just that I'd been with Johnny Diamond when he died and that I had amnesia."

"Give him the slip and meet me here."

"I—I can't do that."

"Do it, or everyone you care about is going to pay the price. We just attached another tracker to his car, so if you tell him and he follows you, we'll know. We're also checking your phone when you get here, so don't even think about texting or calling him, or we'll start with your sister's kid."

Caroline clutched a hand to her throat. "How do I

know you're telling the truth? How do I know I even have a sister?"

"I guess you'll find out when you get your memory back—but it'll be too late then."

Closing her eyes, she said, "Okay, I'll meet you, but I don't have a car. Where am I going and how will I get there?"

"Get down to the loading dock of the hospital. You can get there by taking the elevator to the basement level and exiting the door to the right. You don't have to go past the nurses' station to do it. There will be a car waiting for you. Do *not* try to get a message to the DEA agent. We'll be watching and you'll be sorry."

"I'll be there."

"Now." He ended the call.

She glanced at the curtain dividing the beds. How could she get a message to Cole? And what message would she leave? She didn't know who the caller was or where she was going. Had no description of the car, either.

She took two steps to the curtain and yanked it aside, meeting the wide-eyed gaze of the elderly man in the bed. "When a guy comes in here looking for me—and he will come looking for me—tell him I went back to Mexico."

COLE STOPPED TOSSING his phone from hand to hand and checked the time. How much time did Caroline need with a woman in a coma?

He pushed himself off the wall and sauntered to the nurses' station. "My friend's been in with Linda

Gunderson for a long time. Is it okay if I go back and get her?"

"Room 528."

"Thanks."

He checked the room numbers as he walked down the hall. When he reached 528, he opened the door and poked his head inside. The machines connected to Linda hissed and beeped, but Caroline wasn't at her bedside.

He stepped inside, his heart thumping uncomfortably in his chest. She couldn't have left already. He'd been at the nurses' station the whole time. Calling her name, he headed toward the open door of the bathroom and leaned into the small, empty room.

She'd bolted.

"Excuse me." A faint voice floated from the other side of the curtain, and Cole spun around and pulled it back.

An elderly gentleman raised his hand. "She left and she told me to tell you something."

A pulse thudded in Cole's temple. "The woman visiting next door? What did she say?"

"She went back to Mexico."

Cole collapsed in the chair next to the man's bed, pinching the bridge of his nose. "What else did she say?"

"Just that. She came on my side of the room and told me a man would be looking for her and to tell him that she was going to Mexico."

Cole punched his fist into his palm. He'd allowed her to scam him. Had she remembered everything and decided she liked that life better than this one? Did she ever really have amnesia? She couldn't have faked all those emotions…could she?

"That was after her phone call."

Cole's head jerked up. "Phone call?"

The old man pointed a crooked finger at Linda's bed. "She was talking on the phone before she came over here. Crazy talk."

"What kind of crazy talk?"

"Someone trying to kill her. Diamonds. The DEA. Crazy stuff. When she whipped back the curtain and told me to tell you she was going to Mexico, that confirmed it. Crazy."

They'd gotten to her. Cole dragged his hands through his hair. But how had they convinced her to go with them? And where had they taken her?

"Did you hear anything else from the phone call? A place? A name?"

"The only name I remember is Johnny. That's all I got out of it. I didn't hear her mention the name of any place except Mexico, which she said to me after the phone call."

Cole gripped the man's frail hand. "Thanks. You don't know how much you just helped me."

"I hope she's okay. Real pretty gal, but sad eyes."

"She'll be okay."

And he'd go to hell and back to make sure of it.

He left the room and looked up and down the hallway. An exit sign glowed green next to a heavy door. He strode toward it and pushed against the metal bar. It opened onto a stairwell.

He should've checked out the floor before allowing her to go to Linda's room herself. Cole jogged down the stairs until he reached the bottom floor and burst through the final door.

He found himself on a loading dock, and he approached a guy with a clipboard, doing inventory of some boxes.

"Did you see a woman come out this way recently?" As the man's face began to close down, Cole pulled out his badge.

"I didn't, but I just stepped out here." He jerked his thumb to his right. "Try down there. Those two trucks are almost done unloading."

"Thanks." Cole moved to the next truck and flashed his badge at the man signing for a delivery. "Did you see a woman come out of that door in the past fifteen minutes? Average height, long brown hair, slim, black leather jacket and boots?"

The man eyed the badge, ripped off a copy of the form he was signing and handed it to the truck driver. "Yeah, I saw her."

"What did she do? Where'd she go?"

"When she walked down the steps, a car flashed its lights at her and she got in."

"What kind of car? Did you see who was in it?" Cole tipped his head back and scanned the overhang of the loading dock.

"Small, black compact. I didn't see who was in it. Just noticed because usually people don't come out of the hospital this way to get picked up."

"Are there cameras out here?"

"Not yet, but the hospital's working on it."

"Did you see what direction the car went?"

"Can't see from here which way he turned. Just went up to the alley that leads to the side street."

"Thanks." How was he going to track a small, black compact? No license plate. No description of the driver. Cole felt like punching something, or someone.

He made a turn to go back to the front of the hospital and the parking structure when someone yelled behind him. "Hey!"

He pivoted toward the voice, and a guy standing next to the first man he'd talked to waved his arms at him. Cole backtracked.

"Yeah?"

"You're a cop or something?"

"DEA. Why?"

"Joey here told me you were asking about a woman down here in the last half hour."

"That's right. Did you see her get into the car? Do you have any information about the car?"

"I saw her come out of the hospital but I didn't see no car."

"Oh, okay, thanks." Cole's stomach sank. *Back to square one.*

"But you aren't the only one looking for her."

"Oh? Who else?"

"Some local boy, Jason Foster."

"Jason Foster? Quileute? Dating that waitress at Sutter's?"

"That's the one. He was all agro down here, asking me if I saw some chick, where she went. Man, I told that dude if he was getting rid of Chloe to let me know 'cuz I always had a thing for her, you know?"

"What did he do after that?"

"Took off on his Harley."

"Thanks. I appreciate the heads-up."

What did Jason have to do with all this? He'd shown up at the emergency room with a broken hand the night Linda got sick. Cole had seen Jason earlier that same night hightailing it out of Sutter's back entrance, worried and preoccupied.

Cole raced to his car and drove into town. He pulled across the street from Sutter's and went into the restaurant, which was just getting ready for the dinner crowd.

He spied Chloe talking to Bud at the bar and wiping down menus, but better yet, he saw Jason nursing a beer at the end of the bar. As Cole walked toward him, Jason glanced up.

Then he left his half-full beer glass and headed for the back door.

"Jason!" Cole started moving faster, but the younger man took off at a sprint, bursting from the restaurant.

Cole caught him before he got to his bike, and tackled him. Panting heavily, he jerked Jason's arm behind his back. "What do you know about Caroline Johnson? Why were you looking for her?"

"Oww." Jason twisted in Cole's grasp. "I was trying to save her, man."

"Save her from whom? Where is she?"

"From Rocky Whitecotton. They have her at the Kennedy cabin. I—I think they're gonna kill her, man."

THE MAN WITH the tan, leathery skin prodded her in the back with his gun. "We don't go through the front door."

She tripped as she walked around the side of the rustic cabin set practically in the middle of the woods. Did she know this place? Images rushed at her from all sides. Different images from before—lush greenery replaced the arid desert. She didn't have her family with her, but she wanted them.

The man, Vic, knocked on the door in some kind of code, and a lock clicked from inside.

A terrible fear descended on her and she stumbled backward. She didn't want to go inside. She didn't want to see the person on the other side of that door. It was happening again. He would take her, take her away from all her happiness.

The door opened and a dark eye appeared at the crack.

She covered her mouth. "No, no."

Then the door swung open and Vic pushed her inside and she fell on her hands and knees at the feet of another man. She tipped her head back and stared into the lined face of Rocky Whitecotton.

The man who'd kidnapped her twenty-five years ago.

Chapter Eighteen

Rocky smirked. "You remember, don't you? You even remember what you'd forgotten until last year, when you went snooping around and discovered the truth about your real identity."

She got to her feet and faced him, squaring her shoulders. "That my real name is Heather Brice, and you kidnapped me and Kayla Rush and Stevie Carson... and others."

"The three of you were young enough, especially you, that you forgot all about your old lives and old names. You were happy enough at the commune, weren't you?"

"Until we found out about the drug dealing, the crime, the murders."

"We only murdered our enemies, and I was happy to let you all leave when you discovered our...business and disapproved. Your sister has a happy life in Mexico City with her husband and children."

"Because she doesn't know she's really Kayla Rush, has a twin and was snatched from her real family when she was five years old."

"And you wouldn't know that either if you hadn't gone poking around. You were studying to be a nurse. You gave up your lifelong dream to make some crazy journey to Timberline to find yourself. I couldn't let you do it, Meadow."

"My name's Heather."

"You've been Meadow Castillo longer than you've been Heather, and definitely longer than you've been Caroline Johnson."

"Did you send Johnny Diamond to kill me?"

"Just to bring you back home. He was an idiot. He wasn't supposed to use cyanide, just a little something to knock you out, and he ended up killing himself—and losing our drugs and money." Rocky snapped his fingers. "Where's the money?"

"I don't have any money. The DEA played you when they released the information about all of Johnny's money being missing. I took a small amount to make a start somewhere, and I don't even have that."

His dark eyes narrowed and glittered dangerously. "You're quite cozy with the DEA now, aren't you?"

She shrugged. "They don't know anything because I didn't know anything. They certainly don't know you're here."

"That's supposed to make me feel better? I gathered children from five different states and the kidnappings were never linked. Escaped to Mexico with my new family to start my own tribe of people, and supported my family through my enterprises. I dropped off the radar. The FBI never had a clue where I went and neither did those idiot Quileute who'd banished me from the reservation." He leveled a finger at her. "And you made me come back, put my commune in danger, just to search for a family who's forgotten all about you."

James Brice's sad face flashed across her mind, and his comment that his parents never spoke of the kidnapping and couldn't bring themselves to return to Timberline to sell the last of their property here echoed in her brain.

He was her brother. His instincts had been right. She had a family, and she wanted to get back to them.

She shrugged. "Then let's just go. I suppose you snuck across the border, undetected, and we'll have to return to Mexico the same way. I have no ID, no passport."

"What happened to it? When reports first started coming back from Vic here that you had amnesia, I couldn't figure out why you just didn't look at your passport."

"Johnny must've done something with my purse and everything in it. It was nowhere to be found. I had nothing."

Rocky slapped Vic on the back. "I should've sent you to find Meadow. You did a better job than Johnny."

She stepped back. "He murdered my therapist. He assaulted my friend."

"Outsiders, Meadow. Come back with us now and forget this life. You have your brothers and sisters, your nursing studies."

"Not River…or Stevie." Her nose tingled and she swiped at it.

"River died in that motorcycle accident. Nothing we could do about it."

"Is that really what happened, or did he discover that he was really Stevie Carson and had been ripped from his real family?"

"There you go again." Rocky stroked his beard. "Are you going to come home to Mexico and forget all this, or…?"

"Or what? You're going to kill me like you killed Stevie? How many of us are you going to kill? River and I won't be the last to question and figure out how we came to be part of your isolated commune at the edge of Copper Canyon in Mexico."

"I'm hoping the rest will turn out like Summer. She's content with her little family."

"That's because you've always intimidated her, and she was lucky enough to get away from you when she fell in love with Gerardo."

"I'll forgive you everything, Meadow—our drugs and money that we lost, cozying up to the DEA and even dragging me back here from my compound. Come home now and don't breathe a word of any of this to anyone again."

A pounding at the back door made all of them jump, and her heart did a somersault. Had Cole found her somehow? She knew she could never return to Mexico with Rocky. Those children at the compound, her brothers and sisters, all had blood brothers and sisters and parents who were devastated by their loss.

She had to make everyone whole again, had to make herself whole.

Rocky gestured for Vic to investigate the knock, and Vic crawled across the floor and peeked up through the blinds. "It's Jason."

She folded her arms across her midsection. Why was Chloe's boyfriend here?

Rocky was wondering the same thing. "What is that loser doing here?" He nodded. "Get the door."

During her entire conversation with Rocky, Vic had kept his gun pointed at her. Now he held it in front of him as he opened the door for Jason, and she shuffled a few steps toward the front door. Maybe she could make a run for it while he was occupied with him.

Vic growled. "What the hell do you want? We don't need no more supplies. We're heading out tomorrow."

"Jason?" She hugged herself. "What are you doing here?"

"I—I've been helping Rocky. I'm the one who tried to poison you in Sutter's that night. Sorry, but Rocky's like family to me." Jason pulled the door closed behind him and walked across the room toward Rocky. "My uncle Danny worked with him."

Rocky snorted. "Danny turned out to be worthless, just like you. Sent him here to do a job and he ended up blowing the whole cover off my connection with the Lords of Chaos. It's Danny's fault the FBI fingered me as the catalyst behind the Timberline Trio. Now, what do you want?"

"I'm here to warn you. I heard the FBI knows you're here. You'd better make a move tonight." He reached for the front doorknob, and Vic lunged for him.

"What are you doing?"

The back door crashed open and Cole filled the frame, pointing his weapon right at Rocky's head. "Drop the gun, Vic, or your boss dies."

Vic grabbed Jason around the neck. "I'll shoot this little weasel right here and now."

"Get down, Caroline."

She dropped to the floor and scooted out of the way of the two weapons at cross purposes.

"It's over. I called the FBI and the sheriff's department on my way here. You're going to be surrounded in a matter of minutes."

Rocky reached for his waistband and she screamed. "He has a gun."

Before Cole could get a shot off, Rocky thrust the gun beneath his chin and blew his brains out.

He fell to the floor in front of her, and it all ended the way it had begun.

She was staring into the eyes of another dead man.

Epilogue

The press conference ended, and Heather retreated to the hotel banquet room that had served as a refuge for the families. Her eyes misted over as she surveyed the room filled with joyous children and their parents.

Her own parents, Patty and Charlie, and her brother, James, hovered around her as if they thought she'd suddenly disappear again.

Her mother hugged her for the thousandth time since they'd reunited. "I just can't believe how this all worked out. It's an incredible story."

"What's incredible is how James recognized me after all these years."

"I can't tell you how shocked I was when I found out you were Linda Gunderson's cousin and not my sister. I was so sure."

"And you were right. Now I really feel guilty for slamming you against the car." Cole slapped James on the back as he shook his hand.

Her father gripped Cole's shoulder. "In the end, you're the one who rescued Heather, so we can forgive anything that came before."

Linda, fully recovered from the beating, squeezed Heather's arm. "You should've told me the whole story, Heather. Maybe I could've helped you figure out who you were sooner."

"You did enough, Linda. Covering for me resulted in a beating and a poisoning. You need to go away with Louise the next time she takes a cruise."

The host of the TV show *Cold Case Chronicles* joined their group with her FBI boyfriend, Duke Harper, in tow. "Mr. and Mrs. Brice? I'm Beth St. Regis."

Mom smiled and nodded. "I watch your show."

"Did your daughter tell you that I'm going to be doing a special on the Timberline Trio? Happily, it won't be a cold case anymore."

Dad put his arm around Mom. "She told us, Ms. St. Regis, but we're not interested in the spotlight."

"I understand completely. You don't even have to appear on camera, but could I get some contact information for you?"

"Beth." Agent Harper rolled his eyes. "You need to respect their privacy."

"What do you think, Heather?" Her father hugged her close.

"I think it's an important story, and I'm sure Beth will do a great job. I've already been talking to her."

Beth mouthed a thank-you.

"I don't see the harm, Dad." James smiled at Beth. "Are you at that table over there?"

Her family wandered away with Beth, and Heather grinned at Cole. "She can get anyone talking."

A man with black hair and an intense stare limped

across the room toward them, a beautiful Native American woman hanging on to his arm.

"Heather? I'm Jim Kennedy, and this is Scarlett Easton. I just wanted to personally apologize to you for the role my father played in the kidnappings."

"Oh, please. No apology is necessary." She gestured to Cole. "This is Cole Pierson with the DEA."

Cole shook Jim's hand. "I heard the story about how you and Scarlett dug into the case and made the connection between Rocky and the Lords of Chaos. You're the ones who put the FBI on Rocky's trail and got him on our radar."

Cole turned to Scarlett. "And your cousin Jason helped me stop Rocky."

Heather said, "I don't know if I would've been able to put the final pieces of the puzzle together if I hadn't read an online article about the two of you and the work you did."

Scarlett hugged her in a warm embrace. "I'm so glad you found your way back home, and look at all these people you've been able to reunite with their families."

"You know, Jim, we all lived with Rocky for years and looked at him as a father figure," Heather murmured. "I knew even as a child that he was a bad person, but as children we're trapped. We don't have many choices, but it sounds like you made the right ones."

"Yeah, and some of us are lucky enough to find our real families." He put his arm around Scarlett and kissed the side of her head. "If any of those kids, your commune brothers and sisters, need help coping, give me a call. I work with vets who have PTSD and I have a lot of referrals."

"I'll keep that in mind."

When they left, Cole cranked his head from side to side. "This is turning into quite a party. Even the Timberline sheriffs and the FBI are having a good time."

Heather tugged on his sleeve. "You haven't met Summer—I mean Kayla—yet. Here she comes with her twin."

Kendall Rush wrapped Heather in a bear hug. "I am so grateful to you for bringing my sister back to me."

Kayla smiled shyly. "Now I have two sisters, because you'll always be my sister, Meadow. I'm sorry— Heather."

She smiled. "Cole, this is my sister, Kayla, and her husband, Gerardo."

Everyone shook hands, and remembering all the different names was getting to be a challenge.

Kendall introduced her fiancé, Cooper Sloane.

As Cole shook his hand, he said, "The Timberline Sheriff's Department still talks about you—best sheriff the town ever had. Any chance you'll come back?"

"Not a chance. Neither my fiancée nor my daughter can take the rain. We'll be staying in Phoenix."

Kendall looked around the room. "This is such a happy occasion, except we're missing someone. Did Stevie have a good life?"

"Rocky, as much as he tore apart other families, did it all to establish his own tribe, as he called us," Heather answered. "Despite his criminal activities, he treated us all with kindness. It was a commune—we were isolated and didn't have a lot of modern conveniences, but we learned to depend on each other and we all had our jobs. River, as we knew him, loved working with machinery. He loved dirt bikes and motorcycles. I'd say he was happy, wouldn't you, Summer?"

"I think he was, as much as any of us were."

Kendall put her arm around her twin's waist. "I know you and Gerardo have a life in Mexico, but we're going to visit as soon as we can and you have to come up for our wedding."

As the crowd began to thin and her parents retired to their hotel room with James, Heather turned to Cole.

"For one terrifying week, I didn't have a name or a family or an identity. Now I have three names, more family than I can visit in twenty Christmases and I know who I am."

"Quite a turnaround."

"But through all the darkness, I had one shining light—you."

"I was your shining light, really? Because I was pretty sure you couldn't wait for me to leave Timberline."

She grabbed the lapels of his jacket. "That's just because I didn't know if you were a drug dealer out to kill me or a cop out to arrest me, and you turned into my white knight out to save me."

Cupping her face with his hand, he whispered, "Now you just have too much damned family around. How am I ever going to get you alone again, Caroline, Meadow, Heather?"

"I'll tell you what, *señor*. I have to go down to Mexico to take care of some business. I'm sure you can make up some reason why you need to be down there. We could sneak away, drink tequila, take long siestas.

He nuzzled her ear. "Do we really have to take a nap during the siesta, or can we do…other things?"

"Oh, we can do other things, but will all the excitement go out of it for you now that I'm no longer a woman of mystery?"

"I don't want a woman of mystery. I plan to find out every little detail about you, but don't leave me if I happen to call out Caroline in the throes of passion."

"Leave you, Cole Pierson? Never going to happen."

Then he kissed her and she knew exactly who she was.

* * * * *

COMING NEXT MONTH FROM

♦ HARLEQUIN®
™

I N T R I G U E

Available November 22, 2016

#1677 CARDWELL CHRISTMAS CRIME SCENE
Cardwell Cousins • by B.J. Daniels
Dee Anna Justice doesn't know what to make of private investigator Beau Tanner and the Cardwell family, who seem ready to welcome her with open arms. Her convict father says she needs to be protected from a deadly threat—but can she bring down her walls and let Beau in?

#1678 INVESTIGATING CHRISTMAS
Colby Agency: Family Secrets
by Debra Webb & Regan Black
Lucy Gaines walked away from sexy billionaire Rush Grayson before—the man who has it all seems to have no capacity for love. But when Lucy's sister and nephew are kidnapped, Rush is the only one who can save them and bring her family home for Christmas.

#1679 KANSAS CITY COUNTDOWN
The Precinct: Bachelors in Blue • by Julie Miller
Detective Keir Watson has seventy-two hours to identify the man terrorizing attorney Kenna Parker. Her amnesia makes identifying her stalker difficult. But trusting his growing feelings for the older woman? Impossible.

#1680 PHD PROTECTOR
The Men of Search Team Seven • by Cindi Myers
Nuclear scientist Mark Renfro has been kidnapped by a terrorist cell planning to detonate a nuclear bomb. On the verge of hopelessness, he meets Erin Daniels, the stepdaughter of his captor, whose life is also on the line. Only by working together can they escape, and the clock is ticking...

#1681 OVERWHELMING FORCE
Omega Sector: Critical Response • by Janie Crouch
Joe Matarazzo is the best hostage negotiator Omega Sector has ever seen. But when his ex-lover, lawyer Laura Birchwood, is in a stalker's sights, the situation may be more than even he can handle.

#1682 MOUNTAIN SHELTER
by Cassie Miles
When an international assassin targets neurosurgeon Jayne Shackleford, it's up to Dylan Simmons to keep her safe. A bodyguard and tech genius, Dylan understands Jayne's emotional isolation, and his safe house in the mountains just might have her letting down her defenses.

YOU CAN FIND MORE INFORMATION ON UPCOMING HARLEQUIN® TITLES, FREE EXCERPTS AND MORE AT WWW.HARLEQUIN.COM.

HICNM1116

SPECIAL EXCERPT FROM

⊕ HARLEQUIN®

I N T R I G U E

DJ is about to gain a whole new family in order to escape the danger closing in from all sides in the latest addition to the Cardwell family saga.

Read on for a sneak preview of
CARDWELL CHRISTMAS CRIME SCENE,
the latest title from
New York Times *bestselling author B.J. Daniels.*

DJ Justice opened the door to her apartment and froze. Nothing looked out of place and yet she took a step back. Her gaze went to the lock. There were scratches around the keyhole. The lock set was one of the first things she'd replaced when she'd rented the apartment.

She eased her hand into the large leather hobo bag that she always carried. Her palm fit smoothly around the grip of the weapon, loaded and ready to fire, as she slowly pushed open the door.

The apartment was small and sparsely furnished. She never stayed anywhere long, so she collected nothing of value that couldn't fit into one suitcase. Spending years on the run as a child, she'd had to leave places in the middle of the night with only minutes to pack.

But that had changed over the past few years. She'd just begun to feel…safe. She liked her job, felt content here. She should have known it couldn't last.

The door creaked open at the touch of her finger, and she quickly scanned the living area. Moving deeper into the apartment, she stepped to the open bathroom door and glanced in. Nothing amiss. At a glance she could see the bathtub, sink and toilet as well as the mirror on the medicine cabinet. The shower door was clear glass. Nothing behind it.

That left just the bedroom. As she stepped soundlessly toward it, she wanted to be wrong. And yet she knew someone had been here. But why break in unless he or she planned to take something?

Or leave something?

Like the time she'd found the bloody hatchet on the fire escape right outside her window when she was eleven. That message had been for her father, the blood from a chicken, he'd told her. Or maybe it hadn't even been blood, he'd said. As if she hadn't seen his fear. As if they hadn't thrown everything they owned into suitcases and escaped in the middle of the night.

She moved to the open bedroom door. The room was small enough that there was sufficient room only for a bed and a simple nightstand with one shelf. The book she'd been reading the night before was on the nightstand, nothing else.

The double bed was made—just as she'd left it.

She started to turn away when she caught a glimmer of something out of the corner of her eye.

Don't miss CARDWELL CHRISTMAS CRIME SCENE by B.J. Daniels, available December 2016 wherever Harlequin® Intrigue books and ebooks are sold.

www.Harlequin.com

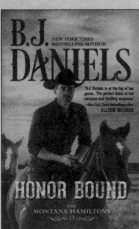

B.J. DANIELS

New York Times BESTSELLING AUTHOR

> "B.J. Daniels is at the top of her genre. The perfect blend of hot romance and thrilling suspense."
> —*New York Times* bestselling author ALLISON BRENNAN

HONOR BOUND

THE
MONTANA HAMILTONS

$7.99 U.S./$9.99 CAN.

THE WORLD IS BETTER WITH

Romance

Harlequin has everything from contemporary, passionate and heartwarming to suspenseful and inspirational stories.

Whatever your mood, we have romance when you need it, wherever you are!

⊞ HARLEQUIN®

A *Romance* FOR EVERY MOOD™

www.Harlequin.com

#RomanceWhenYouNeedIt

Reading Has Its Rewards
Earn **FREE BOOKS!**

Register at **Harlequin My Rewards** and submit your Harlequin purchases from wherever you shop to earn points for free books and other exclusive rewards.

Join for FREE today at **www.HarlequinMyRewards.com**.

HSHMYBPA2016